"Yes, I'd like to go as soon as possible in case Caitlin—"

"Caitlin will be fine," Matt broke in. With a little edge to his voice, he added, "You sound concerned enough to be her mother rather than just her nanny."

It seemed his mood had swung back to wanting to hurt, rather than comfort. "As her nanny, I'm *paid* to be concerned."

"You're paid to give satisfaction—*jobwise*, that is. Though last night you were eminently successful in other fields," he added sardonically, and watched the heated color rise into Caroline's cheeks.

Biting her tongue, she held in check the angry retort she wanted to make. It would do no good to start a fight....

Dear Reader,

A perfect nanny can be tough to find, but once you've found her you'll love and treasure her forever. She's someone who'll not only look after the kids but could also be that loving mom they never knew. Or sometimes she's a he and is the daddy they are wishing for.

Here at Harlequin Presents we've put together a compelling new series, NANNY WANTED!, in which some of our most popular authors create nannies whose talents extend way beyond taking care of the children! Each story will excite and delight you and make you wonder how any family could be complete without a nineties nanny.

Remember—Nanny knows best when it comes to falling in love!

The Editors

Lee Wilkinson is a gifted storyteller whose dramatic stories are full of twists and turns and will keep you guessing to the very end.

Look out next month for:

The Love-Child by Kathryn Ross (#1938)

LEE WILKINSON

The Secret Mother

Harlequin Books

TORONTO • NEW YORK • LONDON
AMSTERDAM • PARIS • SYDNEY • HAMBURG
STOCKHOLM • ATHENS • TOKYO • MILAN
MADRID • WARSAW • BUDAPEST • AUCKLAND

ISBN 0-373-11933-X

THE SECRET MOTHER

First North American Publication 1998.

CHAPTER ONE

FROM the window of her small sitting-room, adjoining the nursery, Caroline watched the snow falling on Morningside Heights. Soft, feathery flakes, swirling from a night sky, piled up against the glass and wrapped the trees in a white shroud.

All at once she shivered.

Snow always made her remember. Brought back the past with cruel clarity. But as the years went by surely the hurt would grow less, the emotional scars heal as the physical ones had?

The mirror no longer showed any sign of them, and even her sensitive fingertips could find no trace. True, she still looked hollow-cheeked, older than her years, but ironically, with her remodelled face, she was almost beautiful now, whereas before she had been merely attractive.

A tap at the door broke into Caroline's thoughts.

'I hope I'm not disturbing you?' Lois Amesbury, her employer, was always scrupulously polite, as well as being pleasant and friendly. 'Only I thought you should know things are finally settled. My husband needs to take up his post at Burbeck Hospital before the new year, so we'll be moving to California during the Christmas break...'

Their decision to move back to the west coast had been mentioned and discussed previously, but Caroline had tried not to think about it.

It was more than two years since the Amesburys had taken a chance, after hearing a little of her story, and

employed the quiet, sad-eyed woman to be nanny to
their twin girls, now three years old.

She was established here, secure, and, if not happy,
she was at least relatively content. The move meant an
upheaval, a parting Caroline had been dreading.

'I'll miss New York,' Lois went on, taking the chair
opposite, 'but I'm looking forward to practising law in
Oakland, and we'll be virtually next door to my folks.
Mom can't wait to take charge of the children...'

*Children that had helped to fill Caroline's empty arms
and empty heart.*

'Though I have a sneaking suspicion she'll spoil them
rotten—' Suddenly glimpsing the desolation the younger
woman was trying hard to hide, Lois broke off abruptly.

After a moment she went on with a practical air,
'What I really came to tell you was, this afternoon Sally
Danvers rang me at the office to ask if you would be
looking for another situation. She knows of a wealthy
businessman who needs a reliable nanny and is willing
to pay top rates.

'There's one child, a girl of about the same age as my
two. Her father is either a widower or a divorcé; I'm not
sure which. Not that it matters... The little girl's grandmother had been taking care of her, but a few months
ago the old lady died quite suddenly.

'I gather the nanny who took over then couldn't win
the child's confidence. The poor little mite didn't like
her, and preferred to stay with the housekeeper. When
her father discovered how things were he asked the
woman to leave, so he needs someone trustworthy who
can start immediately. He'll be home tomorrow morning
if you would like time off to go and see him.'

'Oh, but I can't start *immediately*...'

Lois, dark-haired and elegant, waved away the protest.
'I cleared my office desk today and I'll be at home until
we move, so if you decide to take the job, I'm sure I

can manage. You've been an absolute godsend, and I'm very grateful. That's why I'd like to see you happily settled before we leave.

'The man's name is Matthew Carran. He lives in the Baltimore building on Fifth Avenue. I've written the address and the telephone number on here...'

She passed over a folded sheet of paper.

'Well, I guess I'd better hurry. We've tickets for a concert at the Octagon Hall, if the snow's not too bad...'

But, though Caroline had automatically accepted the piece of paper, she'd heard nothing since the name *Matthew Carran*.

Shock had made the blood drum in her ears and brought a hovering darkness that threatened to swamp her. As the door closed behind her employer she swayed forward and put her head between her knees.

After a moment or two the faintness passed and she sat upright. Talk about the irony of fate! It was almost unbelievable that the man who needed a nanny so urgently should be the one man she couldn't possibly work for.

Or was it the same man? The address was different.

Yes, it *had* to be. Matthew was a fairly common name, but Carran wasn't, and in a way the rest fitted... The last time she had heard, his stepmother had been looking after his baby daughter and he'd been about to get married. But now it seemed he was either widowed or divorced, and with the death of his stepmother the child was left to the care of a nanny.

With a sudden feeling of anguish, Caroline recalled Lois Amesbury saying, 'I gather the nanny who took over then couldn't win the child's confidence. The poor little mite didn't like her.'

Closing her eyes tightly, oval nails biting into her palms, Caroline fought the urge to weep. If only her own circumstances had been different, but in a matter of weeks she would have no home and no job, so there was nothing she could do.

Or was there? Matthew wouldn't recognise the name Caroline Smith. When she had known him she had called herself Kate Hunter. And there wasn't much chance of him recognising *her*.

Though, after this length of time, she should have been used to the metamorphosis, it still occasionally came as a shock to catch sight of a strange woman looking back at her from the mirror.

At twenty-two she had been a good eighteen pounds heavier, and had worn her hair short and blonde and curly. Now it was long and straight, back to its natural ash-brown.

Then she had been young and fresh and curvaceous. Now she was old, if not in years at least in experience, and thin to the point of gauntness, her glow extinguished.

No, he wouldn't recognise her. After several sessions of plastic surgery, it was doubtful if her own mother would have known her.

But it was a risk she couldn't afford to take. She could still see his expression, the way he'd looked at her with such contempt and condemnation.

Still the longing to see him again, the *need* to see his child, was like a physical pain.

No. No! She couldn't do it. Such a step would be utter madness. It would tear open all the old wounds and destroy what little peace of mind she had managed to find.

But if she got the post as nanny it would be the answer to all her prayers.

Fifth Avenue, on this cold, bright morning, was teeming with both traffic and pedestrians, its glittering shops and gilded window displays rivalling the sunshine.

The sidewalks were clear of snow, except where it

had been piled along the edges in dirty banks, but Central Park looked like a winter wonderland, and there was skating on the pond and at the Rockefeller ice rink.

The Baltimore building, she discovered, overlooked the park. Standing in its marble-floored foyer, beneath a magnificent chandelier, Caroline admitted that she'd been insane to come. She was behaving like an utter fool. Yet, lured by the chance to achieve her heart's desire, she had been unable to help herself.

Following a virtually sleepless night, that morning, after she had given the twins their breakfast, she had dialled the number Lois Amesbury had written down and waited with a wildly beating heart to hear Matthew's voice.

It had been something of an anticlimax when the call had been answered by a woman with an Irish brogue, who'd identified herself as Mr Carran's housekeeper.

Caroline had stated her business, and after a minute or so the housekeeper had returned to say cheerfully, 'Mr Carran will be pleased to see you at nine-thirty, Miss Smith. He said to take a cab, and he will reimburse you.'

Hoping that the exercise would calm her, and with time to spare, Caroline had paid off the cab some blocks away, and walked down Fifth Avenue.

Now it was almost nine-thirty and, moving towards the bank of elevators on the far side of the foyer, she was forced to admit that the strategy had failed. Her stomach was churning and she felt almost sick with nerves as she pressed the button for the penthouse suite on the sixty-fifth floor.

As the high-speed elevator carried her smoothly up-wards she took a pair of heavy, dark-rimmed spectacles from her bag and put them on.

Though they were no longer necessary to mask the scar that had run across the bridge of her nose and above one eye, she still preferred to wear them. They were something to hide behind. And knowing the tinted lenses altered the colour of her eyes, changing them from a light, clear aquamarine to a deeper cloudy blue, now provided an added crumb of much needed confidence.

The buxom, middle-aged housekeeper opened the door to Caroline's ring, and hung her coat on the mirrored hallstand.

'Mr Carran is waiting for you in his study,' she said, her smile approving of the newcomer's neat bun, the plain woollen dress and simple calf-length boots. 'It's the door there, on the left.'

Crossing the large, luxuriously carpeted hall on legs that shook, Caroline knocked and waited.

'Come in.' After almost four years, that decisive, low-pitched voice was heartbreakingly familiar.

She swallowed hard, and her palm, damp with cold perspiration, slipped on the doorknob, making her fumble, before the door opened into a book-lined study.

Matthew Carran was sitting behind a polished desk, a slim gold pen in his hand and a sheaf of papers in front of him. As though impatient of the business suit he was wearing, he had discarded his jacket and loosened his tie. His shirtsleeves were rolled up, exposing lean, muscular arms, sprinkled with dark hair.

At her entrance he rose to his feet and stood stock-still, neither moving nor speaking, while his eyes travelled slowly over her.

He seemed taller, his shoulders beneath the pinstriped shirt even broader than she remembered, but his tough, hard-boned face, the peat-dark hair and handsome green-gold eyes were the same.

Though she had thought herself prepared, a flood of emotion swept over her, sending her mind reeling. The book-lined room began to whirl hideously, and the faintness she'd felt the previous evening returned, threatening to engulf her.

Head bent, she bit her soft inner lip savagely, focusing her attention on the pain, refusing to be dragged under.

'Are you all right?' he demanded.

'Yes...' Lifting her head, she swallowed, tasting the slight saltiness of blood. 'Quite all right, thank you.'

'Perhaps you'd like to sit down?'

When, thankfully, she sank onto the chair placed opposite his, he resumed his own seat and remarked with what sounded like genuine concern, 'You're rather pale. Have you been unwell?'

'No.' It was the truth, and she left it at that.

'Have you had much time off while working for Mrs Amesbury?'

'It was agreed that I should have one day a week and every alternate weekend—plus the odd evening, if and when I wanted it.'

But she had rarely taken advantage of the concessions.

'I meant for illness and suchlike.'

'None. I'm perfectly fit and healthy.' *Now.*

He studied the delicate oval of her face for a moment, then gave a slight shrug before saying, 'If you are contemplating working for me we need to get to know each other, so can I ask you to begin by telling me about yourself?'

Before she could comply, he added, 'You have an attractive voice, but you sound more English than American.'

Caroline stiffened. She had given no thought to her voice or her accent.

As she hesitated he asked a trifle impatiently, 'Well, are you English?'

'I was born in London, but I have dual nationality.'

'Tell me about your parents.'

She glanced at him in surprise.

'A person's background can be relevant.'

He'd known nothing of her background previously, so it couldn't do any harm.

'My father, a native New Yorker, was a writer and journalist. He was working in London when he met and teamed up with my mother, who was a newspaper photographer. They got married and I was born a year later. We lived in London until I was fifteen, then we moved to New York.'

'You're an only child?'

'Yes. Having no brothers or sisters is my one regret.'

'So you had a happy childhood?'

'Very. It was slightly bohemian, I suppose. But I always felt well loved and cared for.'

'Do your parents still live in New York?'

Caroline shook her head. 'They were freelancing, covering a fire at a chemical plant in New Jersey, when they were killed in an explosion.'

'How long ago was that?'

'While I was in my final year at college.'

'May I ask how old you are now?'

She hesitated, then answered, 'Nearly twenty-six,' and saw by his face that he'd put her down as considerably older.

'And you've been a children's nanny how long?'

'Since leaving college.' She felt guilty that it wasn't the truth, but it might save him digging any deeper.

Matthew Carran's green gaze probed her face. His eyes had always had the power to warm or freeze. Now, as though he had guessed she was lying, they could only be described as glacial.

After a moment he changed tack to ask, 'Does your present employer insist on you wearing a uniform?'

'No.' Lois Amesbury had been happy to keep things informal.

'Would you have any objection to wearing one?'

Disliking the idea, but aware that it would be unwise to say so, Caroline bit her lip before answering, 'No.'

'What made you decide to become a nanny?'

'I like children.' That was the truth. She had always had an affinity for children.

His tone silky, he suggested, 'So perhaps you regard being a nanny as an easy way of earning a living?'

Stung, she retorted, 'I've *never* thought of it like that... And being a nanny is *not* an easy way of earning a living. It just happens to be the work I prefer.'

After staring at her for what seemed an age, but could only have been seconds, he asked with a twist to his chiselled lips, 'What qualifications have you, apart from "liking children"?'

Flushing, she said, 'I've passed all the prescribed courses in child care and development, diet and first aid.'

'What do you think are the two most important things in a young child's life?'

She answered immediately. 'Security and affection.'

For an instant he seemed to be gripped by some powerful emotion, then it was gone, leaving his lean, dark face devoid of expression.

Unwilling to meet his eyes, Caroline stared at his hands. He had good hands. Lean, well-shaped, masculine hands, with long fingers and neatly trimmed nails.

All at once, going off at a tangent, he queried, 'Do you smoke?'

She blinked. 'No.'

'Drink?'

'No.'

'But no doubt there is...shall we say, a man in your life?'

It was almost as if he was taunting her, and suddenly she found herself wishing passionately that she hadn't put herself through this ordeal.

'No.'

The brilliant eyes narrowed. 'Oh, come now...'

With a flash of spirit, she retorted, 'I hadn't realised that having a man in my life was compulsory.'

As soon as the imprudent words were out, Caroline cursed herself for a fool. Why was she antagonising Matthew Carran when she so desperately wanted this job?

'I can do without the sarcasm, Miss Smith.' His tone was repressive.

'I'm sorry. But surely I'm entitled to a private life?'

'Everyone is entitled to a private life. I just want to be sure yours won't affect your charge. When Caitlin's grandmother died...'

Caitlin, Caroline thought, her heart feeling as though it might burst. They'd called her *Caitlin*.

'...and I had to engage a nanny, I made a bad mistake.' His mouth a thin, hard line, Matthew added grimly, 'I have no intention of making another.'

'If there *was* a man in my life I wouldn't dream of letting it affect any child in my care,' Caroline said quietly. 'But there is no one.'

Tension had dewed her face with a fine film of perspiration, and, feeling her spectacles slip, she pushed them further up the bridge of her nose.

'Why are you wearing glasses?'

His question, coming with the speed of a striking rattlesnake, threw her. 'I—I'm sorry?'

'I asked why you're wearing spectacles.'

'Because I...I need them.'

Rising to his feet, he leaned across the desk and without so much as a by your leave lifted the glasses from her nose. For a long moment, while shock held her rigid, he looked deep into her clear aquamarine eyes.

Whatever he saw in them—anxiety, pain, loneliness, sadness—his own showed not the slightest sign of either pity or recognition.

Caroline gave thanks to whatever guardian angel was watching over her.

Prematurely, it seemed, as a moment later Matthew was raising the spectacles and squinting through the lenses.

He passed them back to her and, as she hurriedly replaced them, queried succinctly, 'Why do you need spectacles that are just tinted glass?'

She stammered out the only answer she could think of, 'I—I thought it would be better if I looked older.'

His voice icy, he remarked, 'Looking older doesn't necessarily make you more suitable.'

Strain had set her head throbbing dully, and, convinced now that he would never give her the job, she felt bleak and hopeless.

Wanting only to escape before those pitiless eyes noted her despair, she half rose. 'Well, if you've decided I'm unsuitable...'

'Please sit down,' he instructed curtly. 'I haven't decided anything of the kind.'

When, the whole of her body shaking, she had obeyed, he informed her, 'While you were on your way here this morning I had quite a long conversation with your present employer...'

He paused, as though deliberately prolonging the suspense, while the seconds ticked away and Caroline fancied she could hear the roar of the traffic far below on Fifth Avenue.

'She told me that you had been with her for over two years, and spoke very highly of you.'

Caroline was just drawing a shaky breath of relief when he asked, 'Who was your previous employer?'

'Previous employer?'

'I mean before Mrs Amesbury.'

Realising too late that, having told him she'd been a

nanny since leaving college, she was in deep water, Caroline floundered. 'Well, I...'

'Surely you remember?' He was giving her no quarter.

She hated to lie but could see no help for it. 'A Mr Nagel,' she improvised wildly as she recalled the plot of a book she'd been reading. 'I took care of his little boy when his wife left him...'

'And?'

'Eventually she came back and they were reconciled, so I was no longer needed.'

Becoming aware that he was watching her hands, moving restlessly in her lap, she clasped them together to keep them still.

'Have you got Mr Nagel's references?'

'I—I'm afraid I don't know what became of them.'

His sceptical look seemed to make it plain that he didn't believe her.

She could feel the guilty colour rising in her cheeks when he said, 'Presumably they must have been satisfactory, or the Amesburys wouldn't have employed you...'

Picking up the pen he'd been using, he began to tap the desk, each little explosion of sound like a hammer-blow, stretching her already overstretched nerves and making her wince.

'Very well, with the proviso that Caitlin likes you, the position is yours, if you want it, for a trial period of one month.'

As she stared at him, pale lips a little parted, he went on, 'Now to practicalities. I'm prepared to allow you the same time off as your previous employer, and if you stay on after the trial period, you will receive two weeks' annual holiday. The post carries a salary of...' he named an exceedingly generous sum '...and there is a self-contained suite next to the nursery, which I think you'll find comfortable.'

When she continued to gaze at him in silence, he observed brusquely, 'You look surprised. Have you changed your mind about wanting the job?'

'No... No, of course not... I just hadn't expected to be offered it.'

'Why not?'

'I...I got the impression you didn't like me.'

Sardonically, he said, 'It hadn't occurred to me that it was necessary to *like* the nanny I engaged.'

As her face began to burn he added flatly, 'If Caitlin takes to you, that's all that matters. She's a sunny, good-natured little thing, and very forward for her age. At the moment Mrs Monaghan, my housekeeper, is looking after her, and according to that good lady the child isn't one scrap of trouble.

'Even so, it's a lot for the poor woman to take on, so if everything goes well, and you decide to accept my offer, I'd want you here, ready to start, by tomorrow morning.'

'Wearing a uniform?' In spite of Caroline's efforts to speak smoothly, there was a ragged edge to the question.

After a moment's deliberation, Matthew answered coolly, 'I think not.'

His tawny eyes on her face, he went on, 'Now, before we go any further, maybe you'd like to ask me some questions?'

When, wits scattered, she failed to respond, he suggested trenchantly, 'Or possibly you already know everything you need to?'

Taking a deep, steadying breath, she managed, 'I just know what Mrs Amesbury told me.'

'And what did Mrs Amesbury tell you?' He sounded annoyed, as though he suspected they'd been gossiping about him.

'Only that you are either widowed or divorced, and your daughter is about three years old.'

'Not terribly accurate, I'm afraid. I'm neither widowed nor divorced…'

So he must be still married… Married to Sara…

Watching Caroline's eyes widen behind the tinted
glasses, he continued, 'And Caitlin isn't my daughter.
My own mother died shortly after I was born, and when
I was nine years old my father married again. His second
wife already had a three-year-old son. Caitlin is my stepbrother's child.'

Quietly, he added, 'In point of fact I've never been
married.'

'Oh, but I thought—' Cursing her unruly tongue,
Caroline stopped speaking abruptly.

'What did you think, Miss Smith?'

She shook her head. 'Nothing… Really…'

His thickly lashed eyes glinted, and she feared he was
going to pursue the matter, but he let it go and said
briskly, 'Well, if there isn't anything you want to ask
me, perhaps you'd like to take a look at the accommodation and say hello to Caitlin?'

Taking a deep, uneven breath, doing her best to control an almost feverish rush of excitement, Caroline rose
to her feet as Matthew left his chair and walked round
the desk.

At five feet seven inches she was fairly tall for a
woman, but, at an inch or so above six feet, he seemed
to tower over her.

Suddenly she found herself trembling with a new and
different kind of excitement, and, looking up into his
dark face, she was shaken to the core by the depth of
her feelings for him.

After all this time she had hoped, *prayed*, that she
would be able to look at him and see only a man she
had *once* known and loved. A man who no longer meant
that much to her.

But the instinctive knowledge that he was the other

half of herself, the part that made her whole and complete, was still there, as certain and inevitable as it had ever been.

As she stood, dazed and dumb, he suggested smoothly, 'Now we've established that you don't need the glasses, perhaps you'd care to take them off? It seems a shame to hide such beautiful eyes.' The last was added with a certain bite, as though he didn't intend it as a compliment.

Unable to think of a reason for refusing, Caroline took off the glasses and slipped them into her bag, trying not to meet his glance in case he should see all too clearly what she was thinking, feeling.

He opened the door and, a hand at her waist, ushered her across the well-furnished hall and into the living-room.

From the first moment they had met his impact had been stunning, and now his touch—light and impersonal though it was—proved to be devastating, trapping the breath in her throat, making her heart lurch drunkenly and her pulse begin to race with suffocating speed.

Despite its open-plan vastness and elegance, Matthew's apartment had a homely, lived-in air. Several toys lay scattered on the Aubusson carpet, and a wooden rocking horse, ridden by a large, floppy rag doll with yellow plaits, stood in front of the long windows.

'The playroom and nursery are this way.' They went through a wide arch and across a second hallway. 'And these rooms will be yours if you take the job.' He threw open a pair of polished doors and showed her around.

Fitted with every mod-con, and beautifully furnished, the suite—sitting-room, bedroom, bathroom and kitchenette—was more than comfortable. It was downright luxurious.

She would have taken the job if it had been a rat-infested dungeon. But everything depended on whether Caitlin showed any signs of liking her.

Feeling a kind of dull hopelessness, Caroline wondered how anyone could expect a child of that tender age—a child who had already had one nanny she didn't like—to take to a woman who was a total stranger?

'Now if you'd like to come and meet Caitlin…'

Turning, Matthew led the way to a large, airy kitchen, where Mrs Monaghan was keeping an eye on her charge while making the morning coffee.

Dressed in a long-sleeved cotton shirt and brightly coloured dungarees, the child was busily engaged in tucking a doll into a pram. Looking up at their entrance, she came running over to Matthew and threw her arms around his legs.

Rumpling her dark silky hair, he said, 'I'd like you to say hello to Miss Smith.' Then, in a conspiratorial whisper he added, 'If we're both very nice to her, she may come and live with us and look after you.'

As Caitlin released her hold and turned to stare solemnly at the newcomer Caroline went down on her haunches. Her heart feeling as though it might burst, she smiled shakily at the little girl.

She was a beautiful and dainty child, her skin with the bloom of a peach, her dimpled cheeks still babyish, her long-lashed eyes an exquisite blue-green.

For long moments they looked at each other without speaking. Then in a clear, childish treble, Caitlin asked, 'Do you *want* to come and look after me?'

Caroline found her voice and said huskily, 'I certainly do. You see, I've been looking after two little girls who have to go away, and it would be lovely to have another little girl to take care of.'

After considering this for a second or two, Caitlin turned and trotted away, to return almost immediately with a large brown bear wearing a red and green striped scarf and a pugnacious expression on his heavy-jowled face.

'This is Barnaby.' She thrust the bear into Caroline's arms.

'Well, hello, Barnaby.'

'He's a boy.'

'And a bear of character, I can see. Would he mind if I hugged him?'

Leaning against Caroline's knee, Caitlin confided, 'He likes to be hugged.'

'He also likes a mid-morning nap,' Matthew suggested, with a glance at his housekeeper.

'Well, come along, me darlings.' Mrs Monaghan obediently gathered up the child and the bear. 'Time for a little sleep.'

As the trio departed Matthew put a hand beneath Caroline's elbow and helped her to her feet.

'Thank you.' Trying to hide her desolation, she added, 'I'd hoped to have a little more time with Caitlin.'

'You'll have plenty of time with her once you've moved in.'

Hardly daring to believe her ears, with a wildly beating heart, she asked, 'You mean...?'

'I mean Caitlin liked you.'

'How can you tell?'

Just for a second his green-gold eyes warmed into laughter. 'Only the people she really likes get to meet Barnaby. So, if you want the job...?'

Filled with joy and excitement, she breathed, 'Yes... Yes, I do.'

'Then as soon as we've had some coffee I'll drive you over to the Amesburys' to pick up your things. That way you'll have the afternoon and evening to settle in before you start work tomorrow morning.'

After so much heartbreak, Caroline could hardly believe her good fortune. But even as she rejoiced the voice of caution warned that she mustn't let gladness blind her to the danger of being here.

Every minute spent in Matthew's company added to the risk of betraying herself, so she must stay out of his way as much as possible, and pray that he never suspected who she really was.

CHAPTER TWO

CAROLINE finished tucking Caitlin and Barnaby into bed and said softly, 'Goodnight and God bless.'

'Is Daddy home yet?'

Matthew, who had been away on a business trip for almost two weeks, was due back tonight, just in time for Christmas.

'No, he won't be home until quite late. But if you go to sleep like a good girl, when he gets here I'll ask him to come in and give you a kiss.'

'Tell me the toad story?' Caitlin pleaded. She was getting tired, and her long silky lashes kept drooping.

Heart melting with love, Caroline agreed. 'All right, if you close your eyes while you listen.'

Obediently the child's bright eyes closed, and a small thumb went into her mouth.

Sitting on the edge of the bed, in the pool of golden light cast by the bunny lamp, Caroline began the fairy story that during the last month had become Caitlin's favourite.

'Once upon a time there was a handsome prince...'

'What was he called?'

'He was called Matthew...'

This part had become a familiar routine, with the same question, the same answer, and the same giggles because, on the first occasion, when Caroline had asked, 'What do *you* think he was called?' Caitlin had unhesitatingly chosen the name Matthew.

'Now, poor Matthew had been turned into a toad by a naughty witch, and the only way to break the spell was for a beautiful princess to kiss him. One fine morning, when he was hopping through the forest...'

The story was one from her own childhood, and Caroline knew it off by heart. The words were soothing, familiar, allowing her thoughts to wander...

It seemed incredible that it was only about a month ago since Matthew had insisted on driving her to Morningside Heights to pick up her things.

While he had talked to Lois Amesbury she had packed—her few clothes and possessions going into a single suitcase—and said goodbye to the twins. With the prospect of having Caitlin to take care of, leaving the family hadn't proved to be the wrench it might have been.

Mrs Monaghan had been kindness itself, and Caroline had settled into the penthouse well. To her very great relief there had been no mention of Matthew's former fiancée, and the days had been filled with the kind of happiness she had never expected to know again.

But, while she gave Caitlin all the love and attention the child needed, Caroline was trying not to make the little girl too dependent on her. Always, at the back of her mind, was the knowledge of how uncertain the future was.

It was a blessed relief—or so she'd told herself—that after the first few days she had seen very little of Matthew.

At first he had watched her as relentlessly as a cat watches its potential prey, then, observing that she had won the child's trust and affection, he had left her to it and set about catching up on a huge backlog of work before heading for Hong Kong.

Without his dynamic presence the apartment had seemed curiously empty, devoid of life and warmth and excitement.

While she admitted that she ought to feel safer when

he was away, part of her longed to see him, to hear his voice and know he was close at hand...

'And the beautiful princess said, "Little toad with crooked leg, open quick the door I beg..."'

Seeing Caitlin had fallen asleep, Caroline stopped speaking and, rising softly to her feet, took the child's hand from her mouth and tucked it beneath the duvet, before stooping to kiss the rosy cheek.

As she switched on the monitoring system and turned to the door the tender smile lingering on her lips gave way to a gasp of fright.

The tall, shadowy figure, lounging in the doorway straightened. 'I'm sorry,' Matthew murmured mockingly, 'did I startle you?'

Wondering how long he'd been standing there listening, she stammered, 'I...we...weren't expecting you home so early.'

He was still wearing his dark business suit. His lean face looked a little strained, she thought, as though even his magnificent stamina had been tested by such an intensive trip.

She felt a rush of tenderness, a longing to open her arms to him and welcome him back.

But even as she wished she had that right she saw that his eyes held a glint, a dangerous sparkle that made warning bells ring.

As he moved into the room she attempted to slip unobtrusively past him, her heart thudding, when he caught her wrist. 'Don't go...'

Ignoring her sharp intake of breath, he stooped to touch his lips to Caitlin's forehead before leading the way out of the nursery and into the playroom, where a single shaded night-lamp burnt. 'We have some unfinished business.'

'Unfinished business?' Alarmed by his air of intent,

the build-up of tension she could feel, Caroline made an attempt to free her wrist.

His grip merely tightened, until his fingers felt as though they might crush the delicate bones. Moving closer, he suggested silkily, 'Surely we need the beautiful princess to kiss the poor toad?'

Finding she'd been backed into a corner, and trying not to panic, she said as lightly as possible, 'It's just a fairy story Caitlin's taken to.'

'Ah, but a fairy story has to have a happy ending, and as the leading character...'

His dark face was only inches away. She looked at his mouth, that austere yet sensual mouth, and remembered with stunning clarity what it felt like when it touched hers.

A treacherous wave of heat engulfing her, somehow she managed, 'I really don't think I'd rate as a beautiful princess.'

'You may not rate as a princess, but you're certainly beautiful enough.' All at once he sounded angry, driven.

Terrified of what might happen if he touched her, she begged hoarsely, 'Oh, please, Matthew...'

Ignoring the plea, he took her face between his hands and his mouth closed over hers.

All thought obliterated, her whole being melted instantly, completely, so that without the support of the wall she couldn't have remained on her feet.

His touch, his kiss, was what her heart and mind and body had craved. When finally he lifted his head, it took her a few seconds to gather herself and register that he was breathing as though he'd been running hard.

Knowing he'd only kissed her because he was inexplicably angry, she felt a fierce satisfaction that he hadn't remained totally unmoved.

'Well, well, well...' he drawled, and his voice had a

harshness to it. 'Who would have dreamt such a prim-looking nanny was capable of so much passion?'

Terrified that her uncontrolled response might have stirred memories in him that were best forgotten, she said raggedly, 'Please let me go. You have no right to treat me like this.'

'Can I plead provocation?' He was laughing now, making fun of her. 'Promise never to touch you again?'

'I'd prefer it if you did, Mr Carran.'

'Why so formal? A minute ago you called me Matthew.'

She felt a quick stab of fear. 'I—I'm sorry... I didn't mean to...I was upset.'

He was still holding her face between his palms, and his thumbs stroked backwards and forwards across her cheeks in a movement that was no caress but an expression of his anger.

'Tell me, Miss Smith, if I find it impossible to keep my hands off you, what will you do?'

She wanted to say that she would go, but at the thought of being anywhere else her heart seemed to shrivel and die in her breast.

'Will you leave?'

Somehow he must have guessed that she would never leave of her own accord, she thought agitatedly, and he was deliberately taunting her.

Her voice impeded, she pointed out, 'I don't think that would help Caitlin. She's just got used to me, and a child of her age needs some stability.'

As though the mention of Caitlin had sobered him, Matthew let his hands drop to his sides and stepped back, his expression controlled and dispassionate now.

But, when Caroline would have hurried away to the safety of her own suite, he once again stopped her. 'Don't disappear,' he said briskly. 'I want to talk to you. Have you had your evening meal yet?'

'No.'

'Then we can eat together and talk at the same time.'

Desperate to be alone until she had regained her equilibrium, Caroline made the first excuse that she could think of. 'Oh, but I usually eat in the kitchen with Mrs Monaghan. She might think it strange if I—'

'Isn't Friday her night off?'

It was. Earlier in the day the housekeeper had announced her intention of spending the evening with her married daughter.

His eyes on Caroline's transparent face, Matthew said sardonically, 'However, if you feel more at home in the kitchen, when I've showered and changed I'll join you there.'

He appeared to be back to his cool, disciplined self, and, watching him walk away, she wondered shakily what had provoked that burning display of anger, that need to deride and dominate.

Surely not just the use of his name in a child's fairy tale?

She felt a cold shiver run through her. He had never tried to disguise the fact that he didn't like her, but for that short space of time he had appeared almost to hate her.

Yet he had kissed her like a man who was starving.

As she made her somewhat unsteady way to the kitchen the remembrance filled her with disturbing and conflicting emotions.

Just one kiss, nevertheless it had altered everything. It had destroyed her composure, banished any slight feeling of peace or security she had gained, and reinforced how perilous her being here was.

A meal had been left ready, and while she put the chicken casserole into the microwave and began to set the table she was beset by a different anxiety. What did Matthew want to talk to her about? Her month's trial time was almost completed, so had he decided to get rid of her?

No, surely not. She tried to be practical. He knew Caitlin had accepted her, and he *needed* a nanny.

Then what? Had he somehow discovered who she was?

No, if he had he would have turned her out immediately. She remembered only too clearly the look of loathing on his face that awful night as, white-lipped, he'd said with a fury no less devastating for being quiet, 'I want you out of my house first thing in the morning. I never want to have to set eyes on you again.'

Shivering, she made an attempt to push the painful memory away. It had happened a long time ago, and was part of the past she tried so hard not to think about.

In a way, coming to work here had been madness, but she couldn't regret taking the chance fate had offered her. Yet it left her open to even more heartache, she thought despairingly, if her brief happiness was about to come to an end.

The click of the latch made her jump.

Though she had thought herself prepared, her heart turned over at the sight of him. He had changed into an olive-green polo-necked shirt and casual trousers, and looked both dangerously attractive and formidable.

He had a way of moving, an arrogant tilt to his dark head, an almost feline grace and symmetry that, combined with his extraordinary eyes, had always put her in mind of a black panther. She felt her mouth go dry.

While she removed the casserole from the oven he took a bottle of white wine from the fridge, and, having opened it, he asked, 'Why only one glass?'

'I don't usually drink,' she answered simply.

His eyes clouding with anger, or impatience, he went to get a second glass. 'I know that's what you told me, but just this once I won't hold it against you.'

As he filled the glasses she put a bowl of fluffy rice and a tossed green salad on the table, and took the chair opposite his.

With easy authority, he served both her and himself before picking up his fork.

For a while they ate without speaking, until, needing to break the silence, striving for normality, she asked, 'Have you had a good trip?'

The chiselled lips twisted. 'You sound for all the world like a dutiful wife.'

'I'm sorry. I was just trying to be pleasant.'

'While I'm being anything but?'

Then, with that sudden change of direction which seemed designed to fluster her, he said, 'The day I gave you the job, I mentioned that Caitlin was my stepbrother's child.'

Though it was more a statement than a question, he was clearly waiting for an answer, and she nodded.

'You didn't ask what had become of him.' Watching the colour drain out of her face, leaving it ashen, he added, 'I wonder why?'

Her voice sounding hollow, echoing inside her own head, she said, 'I didn't consider it was any of my business.'

'I'll tell you all the same. It's three years today since he was killed in an accident. That's why I'm in such a black mood...'

As she stared at him transfixed, unable to move or speak, like someone mortally wounded, he added, 'So perhaps you'll forgive me?'

It seemed an age before she was able to say through bloodless lips, 'Of course...I'm sorry.'

He reached to refill the glasses. 'I take it you've had no worries over Caitlin while I've been away?'

Gathering herself, Caroline said, 'No, she's been fine.

She's missed you, of course, and asked about you every day.'

'She calls me Daddy?'

'Yes.'

'I haven't discouraged her, as I'm hoping to legally adopt her.' Then with no change of tone, he asked, 'Have you made any special plans for tomorrow?'

'Special plans?'

'It's Caitlin's birthday.'

He watched Caroline catch her breath while she absorbed the shock.

'I—I didn't realise... No one mentioned it...' Seeing his face harden with unaccountable anger, she stammered, 'W-was that what you wanted to talk to me about?'

'Amongst other things. But we'll deal with that first.'

Her stunned mind trying to cope with the possibilities, Caroline suggested, 'When I take her to playschool tomorrow morning, I'll talk to the mothers of her special friends and see if I can fix an afternoon party, with a cake and—'

'That won't be necessary. Before I went away I arranged a party at McDonalds which includes a cake and a magician and all the trimmings. About a dozen of Caitlin's friends will be there.'

Feeling as though she'd been slapped, Caroline swallowed hard. 'I'm sorry you didn't think to mention it sooner... I haven't even got a birthday present for her.'

'There's really no need for you to give her anything.'

'I'd like to.'

'Very well. If you want to choose something, have tomorrow morning off. I'll be home all day.'

'Thank you,' she said stiffly. Then, trying to sound as if it didn't matter, 'Will you be taking her to the party?'

'Yes, I'd planned to take her. Why? Do you want the whole day off?'

'No. I—I just wondered.'

Getting to her feet, doing her best to hide her disappointment, Caroline cleared away the first course and, when he shook his head at the chocolate tart, reached for the pot of coffee.

As she filled both their cups he asked idly, 'Have you any plans for the festive season?'

'No.'

'Good. I'm intending to spend Christmas away from home...'

Though she knew it was unwise, to say the least, Caroline had hoped to see at least something of Matthew over the holiday. Now, despite the pleasure being with the child would bring, disappointment made her voice a little flat as she said, 'So you want me to stay here with Caitlin?'

'No, I want you both to come upstate with me. I own a country club and health spa on Clear Lake.'

Caroline went icy cold with shock, as though every drop of warm blood had drained from her body.

'Have you ever been to a health spa?'

'No... I—I know nothing about such places.'

'Then it's high time you did. Can you swim?'

Panic-stricken, she lied, 'No.'

'Then this will be an ideal opportunity to have some expert tuition.'

But the idea of going back to Clear Lake, where she'd once been so rapturously happy, filled her with a bleak anguish.

He picked it up instantly. 'You don't seem to like the idea?'

She voiced the only protest she could think of. 'But you're paying me to look after Caitlin, not learn how to swim.'

'By next year Caitlin should be swimming well herself, and it will be useful if you're already experienced and can accompany her.'

He was talking about next year as if he expected her to still be here. Caroline warmed herself with the thought, before objecting, 'But someone would have to look after her while I—'

'"Someone" will. The spa is family orientated. As well as a highly trained staff we have a number of experienced nursemaids and a babysitting service. Last year we started to run a special nursery and a toddler's activity centre. It keeps the younger children engaged and happy and allows parents to give their nannies a holiday—' he gave her a mocking glance '—while they do their own thing.

'The scheme was my suggestion, and I'd like to try it out first-hand.' Smoothly sarcastic, he added, 'That is, unless you have any objections?'

The very last thing she wanted to do was accompany Matthew to Clear Lake, but he employed her, and she could hardly refuse to go.

After watching the changing expressions flit across her face, he queried, 'Well?'

She shook her head. 'No, I haven't any objections.'

'Good, then that's settled. Can you be ready to go straight after the party tomorrow? Caitlin is at an age where sitting in a car can be boring, but if we travel up during the evening, she'll probably sleep most of the way.'

When, late afternoon the following day, they left New York City, fresh snow had been falling for almost an hour. White and clean and crisp, it covered the sidewalks, clung to lampposts and buildings, and formed pointed caps on each set of red and green traffic lights.

But the main routes upstate were clear, and their journey north through the snowy evening in the big four-wheel drive that Matthew had taken in place of his usual Jaguar was trouble-free and comfortable.

As he had foreseen, Caitlin, who had been bathed and changed and tucked into a cosy sleeping-bag, slept soundly, and for the first few miles only the shush of the tyres and the swish of the wiper blades broke the silence.

Caroline watched the swirling flakes without really seeing them, her thoughts on that afternoon's birthday party.

She had dressed Caitlin in the special party frock and matching ribbons she herself had bought that morning, and when Matthew, who had come through to collect the child, had said merely, 'My, don't you look pretty,' she had experienced a surge of relief.

'Can Caro come with us?' Caitlin asked.

His head came up and, sounding annoyed, he asked, 'Why does she call you Caro?'

'I suggested it,' Caroline admitted.

'Wouldn't Nanny have been more appropriate?'

Caroline swallowed. 'I thought she might have called her grandmother that...some children do...'

'*Can* she come, Daddy?' Caitlin persisted.

'Would you like her to?'

The child nodded vigorously.

His green gaze on Caroline's face, Matthew queried. 'Have you anything better to do?'

'No, I'd love to come,' she said eagerly.

Too eagerly, she'd realised later, but she had been so delighted to get the chance to go, she had forgotten to be cautious.

The party had proved a great success. Though if Caroline had known how often Matthew's gaze had remained fixed on *her* rather than on Caitlin, she would have been alarmed.

But she was so taken up with watching the child, her

heart in her eyes, that for her the only flaw had been the awful moment when one of the staff had referred to her as 'Mrs Carran', and she had seen the frozen look on Matthew's face.

As though reading her thoughts, he broke the silence to ask a shade ironically, 'So, did you enjoy the party?'

Warning herself to be careful this time, she answered casually, 'Oh, yes. I've always liked children's parties. Watching their expressions, the way they react, can be quite fascinating.'

'I thought with so many youngsters to keep an eye on you might be sorry you went?'

'Oh, no, I was happy to be there.'

'Though perhaps you should have worn a uniform after all.' There was a sudden bite to his voice. 'The staff thought you were Caitlin's mother.'

Feeling as though she'd been pierced through the heart, Caroline sat still and silent, gripped by a kind of dread, a fear of some impending blow.

But with a swift change of subject, he queried, 'Have you ever been to Clear Lake before?'

Taking a deep breath, she lied, 'No.'

'It's a wonderfully scenic area of woods and mountains and hot springs that's very popular with New Yorkers. That's why I decided to build a health spa there.'

With a touch of derision, he went on, 'It allows the jaded city-dwellers—or at least the ones who can afford it—to relax and be pampered in picturesque surroundings.'

'You sound a little...disdainful...'

'Though I love the lake, I've always found the club atmosphere somewhat cloying—not to say claustrophobic. A couple of months ago, when an old house that I liked in that area came on to the market I decided to buy it. That way, when the renovations are completed,

I'll have somewhere that's really my own to go to when
I feel the need to get away from the city…'

Caroline was just starting to relax and breathe freely
again when he added, 'My stepbrother liked to get away
from the city, too, but he usually stayed in a hotel north
of the lake. He was having a break up there when he
met the woman who became his wife. I gather they
bumped into each other in the hotel lobby. It seems to
have been love at first sight, at least as far as *he* was
concerned… He fairly doted on her…'

Why was Matthew telling her all this? Caroline wondered painfully. It was almost as if he was deliberately
tormenting her.

'Though I imagine he had no idea what she was really
like…'

There was anger and bitterness in Matthew's voice
now, as he added, 'I'm sorry to say Caitlin's mother had
neither scruples nor morals.'

Caroline shivered. It was quite plain that, even after
all this time, Matthew still hated his stepsister-in-law.

Signalling the end of the conversation, he pressed a
button on the dashboard stereo and the plaintive sound
of 'Bridge Over Troubled Water' filled the car.

Feeling drained, emotionally exhausted, Caroline put
her head back against the seat and closed her eyes.

She must have slept for some time, because when she
opened heavy lids they were pulling into the grounds of
the luxury spa complex that she had first seen almost
four years ago.

Then there had been blizzard conditions. Now the
scene was serenely beautiful. Snow covered everything
in a soft white blanket and odd flakes were still drifting
down—a light scattering from what seemed to be an
almost clear sky.

Well-lit roadways spread from the central area, where
a tall Christmas tree hung with sparkling baubles stood

in front of the main entrance. Light spilled from the long windows and lay in pools of gold across the snowy expanse.

Caroline was surprised when, instead of drawing up in front of the steps, Matthew took a road to the left and stopped outside a single-storey chalet-type house, set apart from the rest.

Catching her look of surprise, he asked curtly, 'Something wrong?'

'No... I just presumed that we'd be staying in your apartment in the main building.'

'How do you know I have an apartment in the main building?' The question was quiet but lethal.

'Well, I—I don't, of course... I—I just thought...' Stammering helplessly, she broke off.

'Well, as it happens, you're quite right. I do have a suite of rooms kept for my own use, but there are only two bedrooms—which would have meant you sharing with Caitlin. Or me.'

Watching the burning colour pour into Caroline's pale face, he added sardonically, 'I didn't care for the first option, and I thought you might not care for the second.'

Opening the car door, he got out, his feet crunching on the fresh snow. Alarmed and disturbed by his black mood and her own stupid blunder, she followed him.

Strapped into the car seat she shared with Barnaby, Caitlin was still sleeping soundly. Lifting her out with care, Matthew carried the child and bear into the chalet and through to a small, cosy room fitted out as a nursery. Then, while Caroline tucked the pair into bed, he went outside again to deal with the baggage.

When she had switched on the monitoring system and turned the nightlight down low, Caroline kissed the little girl's sleep-flushed cheek before going back to the attractive open-plan living area.

The middle of the room was sunken, and a couch piled

with soft cushions queened it in front of a copper-canopied central fireplace, where a log fire blazed merrily. To one side was an all-mod-cons kitchenette, its fridge well stocked with food.

Caroline took off her coat and hung it behind one of the sliding doors in the hallway, her thoughts still in a turmoil. She had expected to be in a hotel atmosphere, surrounded by people, and the idea of being alone here with Matthew was both wonderful and disturbing.

Not to mention *dangerous*. Since he'd returned from his trip his mood had been so strange and intense. So quietly explosive.

She remembered his, '...if I find it impossible to keep my hands off you...' and shivered. He would only have to kiss her, touch her, and she would be lost...

When they'd first met, though she'd been already half involved with another man, she had looked at him and loved him.

He had fulfilled some deep, primitive need in her, and as she recalled her overwhelming and ecstatic response to his lovemaking perspiration dewed her forehead and made her palms grow clammy.

That depth and intensity of feeling had seemed to be mutual. But, while sweeping her off her feet with a passionate urgency, he'd been kind and caring and heartbreakingly tender.

In the intervening years, however, he seemed to have developed a streak of cruelty, and she didn't doubt that if she gave him the slightest opportunity in his present frame of mind he was capable of tearing her apart...emotionally speaking...

The door swung open and Matthew was back, loaded with luggage, snowflakes melting on his dark hair. He put her case in the bedroom next to the nursery, then went to dispose of Caitlin's things and his own.

It had been a long drive, and, knowing he must be

ready for a drink, Caroline filled the kettle and put it on to boil.

She was spooning coffee into the pot when she heard his footsteps returning, and, glancing up incautiously, she met his eyes. For a long moment they looked at one another in silence.

A drop of melted snow ran off his hair and trickled down his lean cheek. She wanted to lift her hand and wipe it away. Instead she asked jerkily, 'Can I make you some supper?'

'I don't expect you to look after me as well as Caitlin.' His voice was brusque.

Flushing a little, she said, 'It's no trouble, really.'

'In that case, thank you.'

While she made a plateful of cheese and ham sand-wiches he sat on the couch, leaning forward, his elbows on his knees, gazing into the flames. His dark face wore a sombre, brooding look that boded ill for the holiday.

Caroline put the coffee pot and sandwiches on a tray and carried them over to a small table nearby. As she turned away he demanded, 'Where are you going?'

'I'm a bit tired,' she answered awkwardly. 'I thought I'd go to bed.'

'Sit down and have a cup of coffee and a sandwich.'

She shook her head. 'I'm not hungry, and coffee this late will keep me awake.'

'Then stay and talk to me.' It was an order.

Biting her lip, she took a seat on the other end of the couch and asked as levelly as possible, 'What would you like to talk about?'

'You. I'd like to know why you're calling yourself Miss Smith.'

Shock made Caroline catch her breath. Somehow she answered, 'Because it's my name.'

'*Miss*—when you've been married?'

Every drop of blood drained from her face. 'What

makes you think I've been married?' Her voice sounded
high and strained.

'Remember the day I took you to pick up your belongings? While you were packing Mrs Amesbury
showed me a snapshot of you and the twins, taken when
you'd only been there a short time. Perhaps you recall
the one I mean? You were sitting with them on your
knee, an arm around each of them...'

When she merely stared at him, her aquamarine eyes
grown dark with apprehension, he went on, 'Facially it's
not particularly good—you have on those heavy spectacles and your head's bent—but your hands are in fo-
cus, and quite clearly you're wearing a wedding ring.'

She'd taken it off and put it away for good shortly
afterwards.

'So tell me about your marriage,' he pursued.

'There's really not much to tell.' Her voice was brittle
as ice. 'We were both young, and it didn't last long.'

'Where is your husband now?'

About to lie, to pretend he'd left her, Caroline hesitated. Suppose Lois Amesbury had told Matthew what
little she knew?

Her lips so stiff they would hardly frame the words,
Caroline admitted, 'My husband died.'

'So why does a respectable widow need to call herself
Miss Smith?'

'I decided to leave the past behind me and revert to
my maiden name. Now, if you'll excuse me, I really am
tired.'

Before he could make any further move to detain her,
she jumped to her feet and hurried away.

If her precipitate departure was unwise, she couldn't
help it. She had come to the end of her emotional re-
sources and could stand no more.

CHAPTER THREE

AFTER the traumas of the evening, sleep refused to come, and Caroline tossed and turned until dawn lightened the sky and the first bird began to sing. Then, exhausted, she slept heavily for more than an hour, wakening to bright sunshine and the appetising smell of coffee.

When she'd showered and pulled on slim-fitting wool trousers and a cream sweater, she went through to the living area to find Matthew.

A tea towel knotted around his lean hips and a lock of dark hair falling over his forehead, he was cooking breakfast while Caitlin fed Barnaby Bear and herself with fruit and cereal.

His glance flicked over Caroline, taking in her air of fatigue and the shadows beneath her clear aquamarine eyes. 'Good morning.' He sounded relaxed and almost friendly, the black mood of the previous night banished. 'Did you sleep well?'

'Very well, thank you,' she lied, adding, 'I'm sorry I'm up late.'

'No problem,' he returned easily. 'We're on holiday.'

Strictly speaking *she* wasn't, Caroline thought, and bent to give Caitlin her usual morning kiss. As she straightened she caught Matthew's satirical glance and flushed.

He made no comment, however, merely remarking casually, 'Did I mention that the spa has a special swimming pool for beginners?'

As she half shook her head he added, 'I've asked for

our best instructor to be standing by, so that after breakfast you can have your first lesson.'

Dismay filled her. She had hoped to find some way of wriggling out of it, or at least postponing things for as long as possible.

'I haven't got a swimsuit.' Even as the protest left her lips she knew it was useless.

'There'll be a selection waiting for you.' His tone brooked no further argument. 'Don't look so worried,' he added, with a sudden edge to his voice, 'you may find you're a natural.'

As soon as breakfast was over Matthew took Caroline along to the leisure complex, which housed several blue and inviting pools on different levels, as well as a sauna and Jacuzzi.

On a kind of raised dais at the end of the teaching pool was a diving basin, and a group of youngsters were learning to dive, supervised by a tall blonde woman.

Outside it was a beautifully sunny day. Ice had formed lacy embroidery around the edges of the sapphire lake, and the trees looked as if they'd been sugar-frosted, while on the slopes the snow lay thick and even, patterned in parts with animal and bird tracks.

Inside, safe from the rigours of winter, the air was comfortably warm, and a pale sandy beach, complete with palms and flowering shrubs, gave the illusion of a tropical island.

The whole place had a sensuous sybaritic feel, while the poolside furniture and the bar-restaurant, with its palatial changing cabins, could only be described as luxurious in the extreme.

After Matthew had introduced Caroline to the young well-built instructor who was waiting for them, he cast a cursory glance over the swimwear on display, then left her to choose while he took Caitlin and Barnaby over to the toddlers' activity centre.

By the time he returned she had changed into a modest one-piece suit, patterned with oranges and lemons on a white background, and a matching terrycloth robe.

She hoped that if Matthew did intend to swim he would join the experienced swimmers in one of the other pools. Her hopes were dashed, however, when he said, 'You go ahead. I'll join you as soon as I've changed.'

The handsome fair-haired instructor, who'd introduced himself as Brett Colyer, jumped into the shallow water and waited while she walked carefully down the steps.

Caroline had always enjoyed swimming and as the water flowed around her, silky, cool and caressing, she felt her spirits lift.

Once she was in the pool, and looking at her ease, Brett began to demonstrate various strokes. Her attention only partly on what he was saying, she saw Matthew arrive. Dressed in neat black trunks, his olive skin gleaming, his dark hair a little rumpled, he looked disturbingly attractive.

Very conscious of his unrelenting gaze, she tried to behave like a beginner as, following Brett's instructions, she practised first floating on her back and then turning to do a few breast strokes.

When, after some patient tuition, she 'managed' to swim a width, Brett said enthusiastically, 'Excellent progress, Miss Smith. You're obviously a born swimmer.'

Matthew, who had just completed a couple of leisurely lengths, broke in drily, 'I'm very pleased to hear it.' He glanced at his waterproof watch. 'Well, I think that's enough for the moment. Thanks, Brett.'

Caroline added her thanks, and as the instructor left the pool Matthew turned to follow, pausing to say, 'I'm just going to get dressed and check on Caitlin—make sure she's happy.'

'Oh, but shouldn't I do that? After all, it's what I'm being paid for.'

'At the moment you're being paid to learn to swim.' His tone was uncompromising. 'If you want to stay in the shallow end and try another width or two before you get changed, I'll be back shortly.'

Despite the painful memories that had crowded in, just that one awkward width had brought back all her old delight in the sport. She longed to try a really fast crawl, to feel again the marvellous sensation of cleaving effortlessly through the water.

Instead, she was doing graceful but slow widths when she heard a shout and, looking towards the diving basin, saw a young boy standing on the edge peering into the water.

It was clear that something was amiss. The blonde who had previously been supervising the youngsters was nowhere to be seen, and no one else was near.

Caroline completed the width at racing speed and, hauling herself out of the pool, ran to the boy. 'What's wrong?'

'It's my brother...' he blubbered. 'She wouldn't let him dive from the top board, so when she'd gone he sneaked back. I think he's hurt himself, and I don't swim too good...' The words tumbled over each other.

Caroline took a deep breath and dived in, neatly and cleanly. A boy of about nine or ten was just struggling to the surface, choking and gasping.

Seizing hold of him, she instructed tersely, 'Lie on your back.'

He obeyed, and with a hand beneath his chin she towed him to the side. 'Are you all right?' she asked, when she'd helped him out.

'Just winded,' he muttered. 'But Mom will sure give me hell when she hears about it.'

'Don't you think you've earned a telling off? It was a silly thing to do. You could have been badly hurt.'

'Guess so,' he admitted ruefully.

Taking pity at his woebegone face, she added, 'But I don't suppose your mother will be angry for long. She'll be only too pleased you're all right.'

A couple of older boys appeared on the scene. 'Hi, Vincy, you okay?' one asked.

And then the other suggested, 'Want to go down the flume?'

Seeing she was no longer needed, Caroline turned to make her way to the cabin where she'd left her clothes.

At first she could see no sign of Matthew, and she was just drawing a breath of relief when she noticed him standing on the balcony, his eyes fixed on her.

How long had he been there? If he'd seen what had happened he would know she'd lied about not being able to swim.

He descended the steps and came towards her with a long, somehow menacing stride. She was standing tense, waiting for the axe to fall, when he said casually, 'At first I couldn't see you. I thought you might have gone to get changed.'

Bending her head, so he wouldn't see her face, she said, 'I'm just on my way.' Then she added hastily, 'Is Caitlin all right?'

'Happy as a sandboy. I asked her if she wanted to come and have lunch with us, but she preferred to stay and enjoy an indoor picnic with the others.'

'Oh...' Though part of her *wanted* to be alone with Matthew, she knew only too well how hazardous it could be, how many pitfalls she might encounter.

'As we *are* on our own,' Matthew went on smoothly, 'I suggest we drive along the Skyline Parkway and do some sightseeing.'

'Will we be able to?'

'Oh, yes. There are quite a few houses up there, so it's a road that's usually kept ploughed. Though it's not particularly high, you'll find the views from the ridge breathtaking. We can stop on the way for a spot of lunch at Sky Windows.'

When she made no demur, though her heart was beating fast with a mixture of alarm and elation, he added, 'I'll fetch the car and wait for you outside.'

A kind of nervous anticipation was making her all thumbs, but Caroline showered and changed as quickly as possible, blow-dried her hair, and coiled the silky ash-brown mass into a neat chignon before hurrying out to the waiting car.

The air struck cold after the artificial heat of the complex, and a shiver ran through her. Matthew, who was standing bareheaded, his hands thrust into the pockets of his jacket, noticed that betraying movement. Quickly he opened the door and settled her into the passenger seat.

He had left the engine running, and the car was comfortably warm as they began their journey. The big four-wheel drive climbed the snowy flank of the mountain effortlessly, and when they reached the ridge, as Matthew had promised, the views were superb.

But, only too aware of the man by her side, and filled with a kind of suffocating excitement, Caroline was hardly able to enjoy them.

Taking their time, they drove along the Parkway to the Sky Windows complex, which was perched on a plateau.

As well as the revolving restaurant, there was a covered area of high-class shops and bars, and a wide, paved terrace for summer visitors who wanted to sit in the sun to sip a glass of wine. Now the terrace was deserted, and spread with a white, unsullied carpet of snow.

As they left the car to walk the few yards to the imposing entrance Caroline saw that the early-morning brightness was disappearing and the sky was beginning to turn overcast, with clouds gathering low on the horizon.

The circular restaurant appeared to be full, but, having greeted Matthew by name, the head waiter led them to a reserved table by the window.

'A dry martini?' Matthew queried.

Wondering what had made him choose that particular cocktail, Caroline was about to refuse when she thought better of it. Suppose he was trying to trap her?

Keeping her voice level, she said, 'That would be nice.'

Apparently picking up her slight hesitation, he lifted a dark brow. 'Of course, if you'd prefer something else…? I once knew someone who *loathed* vermouth.'

'No, no, I love it,' she assured him mendaciously.

The drinks came promptly, and, trying not to shudder, she sipped while they perused the menu and ordered.

There had been something in Matthew's manner when he'd said, 'I once knew someone who *loathed* vermouth,' that had made her even more uneasy. It had been almost as though he was baiting her.

Tense and wary, feeling as if she'd been caught up in some nerve-racking chess game or battle of wits, she found herself waiting for his next move.

But while they ate an excellent and leisurely meal Matthew kept the conversation light and impersonal, seeming to sense his companion's anxiety, talking knowledgeably about the terrain and the varying weather conditions.

'This area sometimes differs from the more easterly part—' Breaking off, he asked, 'Sure I'm not boring you?'

She shook her head. Relaxed now, happy to listen to his attractive voice and watch his lean, strong-boned face, she could have sat there for ever. 'Why this particular area?'

'Because, like Buffalo, we're close to a lake. We sometimes get freak snowstorms, white-outs that close the roads, trap people in their homes and bring everything to a standstill...'

Unconsciously she stiffened. She knew about the white-outs first-hand. Being caught in one had altered her whole life.

At that moment their coffee arrived, and after it had been poured, eager to change the emotive subject, she asked, 'Have you always lived in New York?'

'My father was in the diplomatic service, and when I was young we moved around the world a lot. I was born in Washington, educated in Oxford, and lived in Paris for a while.

'When I returned to the States I found I liked this area. Now, of course, I come up quite a lot. I brought my fiancée here a few times,' he added casually, 'especially in the winter. Sara is an excellent skier.'

He'd spoken as if Sara was still part of his life.

Her cup halfway to her lips, Caroline froze. She had been working for Matthew for a month and this was the first time Sara's name had been mentioned.

His green eyes gleamed. 'Why so surprised?'

With difficulty, she said, 'I hadn't appreciated the fact that you were engaged.'

'At your original interview I gained the distinct impression that you expected me to have been married.'

'Well, I...I suppose Mrs Amesbury must have put the idea into my head by describing you as either divorced or widowed...'

'As I said at the time, I am neither. Nor, as a matter of fact, am I still engaged...'

Caroline felt a kind of sick relief. Even for the sake of being with Caitlin, she wasn't sure she could bear to stay in his employ and see him married to another woman.

'I was planning to get married, but my fiancée, or more correctly my *ex*-fiancée, changed her mind a few weeks before the wedding.'

Caroline found that hard to believe. Wanting to ask, Why did she change her mind? she bit her lip.

His tawny eyes fixed on the pale oval of her face, Matthew answered the unspoken question. 'One reason might have been that I was hoping to be able to adopt Caitlin after we were married. Perhaps, when it came to the crunch, Sara felt she couldn't take on another woman's child.'

No, no, surely it couldn't have been that!

'You look as if you disagree,' he said, adding caustically, 'But don't forget everyone isn't as fond of children as you are.'

When, feeling flayed, Caroline said nothing, he went on, 'Of course, Caitlin's grandmother adored her. Rather too much so...' He frowned. 'Grace had worshipped her son, and after his death Caitlin was all she had left, so in some ways she smothered the child.

'Even after her first heart attack, when the hospital warned her to take things easy, she still refused to have a nanny and insisted on doing everything herself.'

'Caitlin must miss her a great deal,' Caroline said huskily.

'Young children are very resilient, thank God, and Caitlin's naturally outgoing and independent, but I think she's had enough upheavals.'

He drained his cup before continuing, 'When I asked what you thought were the two most important things in a child's life, you answered, "Security and affection..." Well, I agree with you, and from now on, no matter what it costs—' his face was grim '—I'm determined to give her the stability she needs...'

'More coffee, madam, sir?' an attentive waiter asked.

'No, thank you.' Caroline shook her head.

Matthew glanced at his watch. 'No, just the bill, please.' Then he turned to Caroline. 'I suppose we'd better be moving, or we won't have time for another spot of sightseeing before it gets dark.'

While they had talked and lingered over their meal the restaurant had gradually emptied, and by the time Matthew had paid the bill they were amongst the last to leave.

Outside the brightly lit complex the day was now grey and gloomy. A wind had sprung up, and as they walked back to the car a flurry of fine snow stung their faces.

Few cars remained in the car park, and the ones that were moving all seemed to be heading back.

'Perhaps we'd better go straight down,' she suggested, faintly apprehensive.

He glanced at the leaden sky. 'I think we've time to get to Prospect Point. From there you can see the Bright Angel Falls.'

Though still uneasy, she told herself it would be stupid to argue. Matthew was an expert at judging the weather conditions in this area, so he should know.

By the time they'd reached their goal there wasn't another car in sight. The sky looked even more threatening, and the road was covered in a fresh white blanket.

But even through the snow, which was falling in earnest now, the Bright Angel Falls were spectacular. For a while, standing beneath an umbrella Matthew had produced, Caroline was entranced.

Then, teeth chattering, she said, 'I could stay here for hours, but it must be getting late, and I'm starting to feel really chilled.'

'Yes, I think it's time we were going down.' Matthew

hurried them the few paces back to the car, and, having helped her in, shook the umbrella and folded it before tossing it in the boot.

It seemed a long way as they headed into what had suddenly become a blizzard. A myriad white flakes swirled in the bright tunnel made by their lights, and even the fast, powerful wipers were unable to keep the windscreen clear.

'I think it's getting worse.' Caroline couldn't hide her dismay.

'So it is.' He tutted. 'But you've no need to worry.'

He sounded *unconcerned*.

Remembering the two-hundred-foot drop from the ridge to the valley below, she asked as steadily as possible, 'Wouldn't it be safer to stop?'

'Not just on the road. If the blizzard keeps up for long we could be trapped in the car and freeze to death.'

'Couldn't we find shelter somewhere?'

'I intend to. In fact we're almost there.'

Her heart lifted. 'Sky Windows?'

'No. The whole complex shuts down for the night.'

'Oh... Is there a hotel on the Parkway?'

'Nothing so convenient, I'm afraid.'

'Then where?'

'Remember I told you I'd bought a house in this area? That it's in the process of being renovated...? Ah, here we are...'

The car turned off the road and began to climb. Caroline could see nothing but swirling snow, but after a hundred yards or so Matthew turned into what she guessed was a drive and drew to a halt.

There was no sign of any lights. 'You mean it's empty?' Her voice sounded high and scared.

'At the moment. I took on the former housekeeper and her husband along with the property, but they're visiting their family over Christmas and New Year. Workmen have been in until yesterday. They're in the process of installing a new heating system, so the place will be a shambles. But at least it will be a roof over our heads for the night.'

Barely able to keep the panic out of her voice at the thought of being stranded overnight in an empty house with Matthew, Caroline voiced her other main concern. 'But what about Caitlin?'

'Don't worry; she'll be well looked after. I gave instructions that if it looked like we were going to be back late Gladys, the most experienced nanny at the club, should put her to bed and stay with her until we got back.'

He came round to open the passenger side door, and, having helped Caroline out, put a strong arm around her. She allowed him to lead her into the shelter of a porch.

A key grated in the lock, a welcome light flashed on, and a moment later Matthew had pushed her into a well-proportioned hallway and closed the door against the blizzard.

The house, which appeared to be quite large, was all on one level. 'This way.' He led her into a spacious living-room-kitchen. It was comfortably furnished, and at the far end there was a woodburning stove and an alcove full of logs.

Though it was obviously in the process of being altered, her first impression was that it was a charming room.

Matthew had crossed to the stove and was already setting a match to the kindling and adding split logs to make a cheery blaze.

As she stood, irresolute, he turned his dark head to look at her and said briskly, 'It will soon warm up if you want to take off your outdoor things.'

When she obeyed, he took her coat and, pulling an armchair closer to the stove, suggested, 'Sit down here.

As soon as I've checked which of the bedrooms are habitable I'll make a hot drink. You look as if you could use one.'

She felt trapped and helpless, isolated here with a man she knew disliked her, a man who, nevertheless, had kissed her with a hungry passion and doubted his ability to keep his hands off her.

Shivering, she thought how strange it was that, in spite of her altered appearance and the passage of time, that sexual chemistry should still be so strong.

It had been there from the start, potent, powerful, overwhelming both common sense and an inbuilt reserve. But while he'd felt only desire for her, she had looked at him and loved him.

Whereas all she'd been able to feel for Tony had been affection and an odd kind of pity. She had tried so hard not to think about the past, but now it suddenly seized and overwhelmed her...

Her mind went back to when she'd been a graduate, and on her own after the death of her parents. She had left college with no home and virtually no money, but with the fixed intention of being a nanny.

Known from childhood as Kate, she had found her full name, Caroline Caitlin Smith-Hunter, something of a mouthful when job-hunting. Deciding to drop the Smith—her mother's maiden name—she had called herself Kate Hunter...

Jobs, Kate soon found, were not easy to come by. Though a number of families wanted a nanny, they invariably wanted someone with experience.

A college friend gave her temporary accommodation, but, feeling beholden and in the way in such a tiny, cramped apartment, she finally decided—in desperation and as a short-term measure—to take any job she could get.

Offered a post as part of the live-in administrative staff of the Gresham Hotel at Adoga, just north of Clear Lake, Kate moved upstate.

There, one early November morning, she quite literally bumped into the most romantically handsome man she'd ever met.

Slightly built, with black curly hair, hazel eyes, and a thin, sensitive face, he looked, she thought, like a poet.

He introduced himself as Tony Newman, and invited her to lunch. They got on very well together, and that evening, after she had finished work, he took her to the local theatre.

Those meetings were the first of many.

Though he lived and worked in New York itself, he came upstate almost every weekend, saying he liked to get away from the city.

As she got to know him better she discovered that he was intense and highly strung, with a strain of brooding melancholy running like a hidden stream beneath the surface charm. It made him seem more fascinating and Byronic than ever.

When the festive season approached, he booked into the hotel for Christmas and New Year, so they could spend as much time as possible together, and early in January he asked her to marry him.

She refused, saying it was far too soon to get serious, but he continued to press her by letter and phone, getting more and more importunate as the weeks passed.

On his next visit, when she told him bluntly that she disliked being pressured, he said pathetically, 'I'm sorry, Kate, I've *tried* to be patient, truly I have…'

In one respect, at least, it was the truth, and her anger melted away. As well as being good company, he'd proved to be kind and gentle, sensitive to her feelings.

He'd often held her in his arms and kissed her, but, unlike a lot of men she'd met, he'd never made any attempt to rush her into bed. For that she was grateful. An unpleasant experience, when she'd been barely seventeen, had made her wary of men.

Tony and she were much of a height, and now, leaning his forehead against hers, he pleaded, 'If you'd only agree to at least get engaged...'

Feeling an almost maternal tenderness for him, but unwilling to commit herself when she was so uncertain, she said, 'I'd rather not get engaged until I'm sure of my feelings.'

'If you want to change your mind later, I'll understand.'

Shaking her head, she told him gently, 'I think it would make more sense to wait. For one thing, we know so little about each other.'

'How can we get to know each other better when we live so far apart?' he complained. 'If you'd only come back to New York... You once told me you liked New York.'

'I do. But I have to have a job, and a roof over my head.'

'Look, Big Brother's a property developer, and he must own a sizable chunk of the city...' Tony, who seemed to both resent and be in awe of his elder brother, always referred to him in that way. 'Suppose I ask him to find you a job in one of his hotels or offices? I work for him and we might even manage to be together if he—'

'No, I don't think so,' she broke in decidedly. 'If I did move back to New York I'd want to stand on my own two feet.'

Tony sighed, then asked, 'When is your next long weekend off?'

'Next weekend, as a matter of fact.'

He seized her hand. 'Then come and meet my mother.

Big Brother is away, so it's an ideal opportunity. You can stay two or three days and get to know each other.'

'But will your mother—?'

'Mother will be only too delighted!' he broke in eagerly. 'Ever since I left college she's been nagging me to find a steady girlfriend.'

As Kate wavered he added, 'Honestly, she's just like most mothers. She can't wait for me to get married and give her some grandchildren. *Please* come. She'll welcome you with open arms.'

A shade uneasily, Kate agreed. 'Very well. But don't let her get the wrong idea. This is just a friendly visit. I'm not committing myself to anything.'

On the following Friday she set off for New York City. Mr Wallace, the hotel's manager, and his wife, who was head of personnel, were planning to visit their newly ordained son in Queens, and had offered her a lift.

It was the end of March and still bitterly cold after a particularly severe winter. But the roads had been ploughed and they were making good time when it began to snow heavily.

A brisk wind was blowing, and in a matter of minutes they were driving through blizzard conditions, the wipers struggling to keep the windscreen clear.

It was almost dark, and the headlights were scarcely able to pierce the driving white curtain. They had dropped to walking speed when, muttering something that might have been a prayer, Mr Wallace turned off to the right.

Cutting short his wife's startled protest, he said, 'I think this is the road to the Clear Lake spa complex. If it is, we can probably find a room there for the night.'

'What if it isn't?' Mrs Wallace quavered.

No one answered.

They had crawled some three-quarters of a mile when

lights became visible through the snow, and everyone drew a breath of relief as they pulled up in front of what seemed to be the main building.

When they had grabbed their luggage, they struggled inside to find the place was frankly sumptuous. There was a vast reception area with a richly carpeted floor, innumerable bowls of fresh flowers, opulent furniture and several ornate chandeliers.

Briefly Mr Wallace explained the situation to the smartly dressed woman behind the huge circular desk, adding, 'So, if you've a room for Miss Hunter, and one for my wife and myself…?'

Looking apologetic, she said, 'We can manage a double room for you and your wife, Mr Wallace, but because some of our guests who were planning to leave have had to stay on, I'm afraid we've nothing for you, Miss Hunter. Though of course you're very welcome to a couch in the lounge.'

Kate was about to thank her and say that would be fine when a low-pitched, decisive voice spoke from behind her. 'I think we can do better than that, Miss Deering.'

She turned to see a tall, broad-shouldered man dressed in well-cut casual clothes. His hair was the colour of peat, his thickly-lashed eyes an amazing green-gold.

Though not strictly speaking handsome, he had the kind of tough, attractive face she wanted to keep looking at; it was an arrangement of features that fascinated her and pleased her aesthetic sense.

In addition to his looks, he wore an easy air of power and authority that in itself, she was soon to realise, was a potent aphrodisiac.

'I'm Matthew Carran,' he introduced himself. Then he said to the receptionist, 'Will you get one of the staff to show Mr and Mrs Wallace to their room?'

Turning to Kate, he said, 'If you'd like to come with

me, Miss Hunter?' He bent to pick up her small case, and as he straightened their eyes met and he smiled at her.

It was instant enchantment, as though some spell had been cast. But, if it had, he too was caught up in it. She could see the reflection of her own attraction in his eyes.

Feeling ridiculously flustered and confused, she followed him across the acres of carpet to a door which opened into what appeared to be a luxurious, self-contained suite.

As he led her into an elegant living-room, with what she recognised as a Monet hanging on the wall, she remarked, 'This looks like a private apartment.'

'It is.'

'Yours?' she guessed.

'That's right.' He gave her another stunning smile that made every bone in her body melt.

Common sense warned that, except for maybe a passing attraction, Matthew Carran could feel no real interest in her, and, telling herself crossly that she was being an absolute fool, she tried to pull herself together.

Apart from anything else, he must be nearly thirty, so in all probability he was already married. It was a distinctly unwelcome thought, but one she was unable to ignore.

'Won't your wife mind having an uninvited guest thrust on her?' The words were out before she could stop them.

He half shook his head. 'I'm not married.'

She felt a flood of relief. To hide it, she asked hastily, 'I take it you're the spa's manager?'

'I own it,' he answered simply.

'Oh.' He must be very wealthy. Which put him right out of her class. Biting on her disappointment, Kate decided that it was just as well she knew. That way she wouldn't cherish any false hopes of getting to know him better.

He opened the door into a beautifully furnished bedroom with an *en suite* bathroom. 'I think you'll be comfortable here.'

A thought struck her, and a shade awkwardly she asked, 'You're not giving up your own room?'

'No. My bedroom's the next one along.' A gleam in his eye, he added, 'However, there's a stout bolt on your door.'

Knowing she was being teased, she said as calmly as her wildly beating heart would allow, 'I can't imagine I'll need it.'

He put her case on a carved oak chest and observed, 'You have an English accent?'

'Yes, I was born in England, though I've lived in the States for some years.'

'I gather you were hijacked by the weather. How far have you come?'

'From Adoga.'

'Heading for where?'

'New York City. But there's no way we could have made it tonight.'

'Nor tomorrow, if I'm any judge. It's going to be a white-out. I've just heard a lot of roads are closed, and the phones are already down. Nothing will be moving for at least twenty-four hours.'

By rights she should have been upset, annoyed that her long weekend was being spoilt. Instead she felt a surge of pleasurable excitement to think that she might be staying in Matthew Carran's lavish apartment for another day.

Realising he was watching her face, she said hastily, 'Then it's a good thing we weren't trapped in the car.'

'It happens to someone most winters. If they've taken sensible precautions, they're rescued in time. But for the ones who haven't,' he added grimly, 'help often comes too late.'

She shivered. 'I believe Mr Wallace is an experienced winter traveller, but even so we were extremely lucky to be close to the complex.'

'It beats having to be dug out,' he agreed. 'Now, if you'll excuse me, I've some things to attend to, so I'll leave you to make yourself at home.'

At the door, he turned to ask casually, 'Will you have dinner with me later?'

Her heart missed a beat, and then went racing. 'Thank you, I'd like to.'

'In the meantime please feel free to use any of the spa's facilities. Perhaps you'd like to relax in the beauty parlour—have some aromatherapy or maybe a massage?'

'Well, I...'

'If that kind of thing doesn't appeal to you, and you'd prefer to take some exercise, there's a fully equipped gymnasium and several swimming pools.'

'A swim would be lovely, but I don't have a costume with me,' she said regretfully.

'I'll see what I can do.' He smiled at her and was gone.

It was like switching out a light.

But they were having dinner together. Just that thought held a breathless promise that consoled and filled her with joy.

CHAPTER FOUR

SOME five minutes later, after she had unpacked her toilet things and freshened up, she was in the living-room, studying the shelves of books, when there was a tap at the door.

She opened it to find a young man standing there with a small package. 'Mr Carran asked me to give you this, Miss Hunter.'

Almost before she could thank him, he was gone.

She opened the package to find a superbly cut black swimsuit in exactly her size. Wondering where he'd managed to find it, she went to take a towel from her case.

It was, she discovered on her way to the pool, a large complex, with every facility—including a glittering parade of shops selling a variety of luxury goods and gifts.

One boutique was displaying an eye-catching range of designer swimsuits similar to the one she had with her. They were ruinously expensive.

Though the gym appeared to be fairly busy, there weren't a lot of people in the vast area which housed several blue-water pools.

Kate changed in one of the well-appointed cabins, and almost gasped when she saw herself in the full-length mirror. The swimsuit fitted her slender but curvaceous figure to perfection, and looked sensational.

There were a mere handful of swimmers in the large pool as she dived in and began a leisurely breast-stroke.

She'd done perhaps a third of a length when there was a faint splash and a seal-dark head surfaced beside her.

Matthew Carran's attractive voice said, 'I thought I'd forget business for the rest of the day and join you.'

The shock of pleasure that ran through her was frightening.

'That is, if you have no objection, Miss Hunter?'

Pausing to tread water, she said, 'Of course not.' Her breathing not quite even, she went on, 'Won't you call me Kate?'

'I'd be happy to, if you'll call me Matthew.'

When she thought she had her voice under control, she said, 'I appreciate the loan of the swimsuit.'

'It isn't a loan; it's a gift...'

Flustered, she began, 'Thank you, but I really can't accept—'

'With the compliments of the spa.'

'Oh... Well, thank you.'

Seeing she still looked a little uncomfortable, he added, 'Mr and Mrs Wallace were offered a choice of swimwear too, but, not being swimmers, they preferred to have a complimentary meal in the restaurant.'

For a time they swam in silence, while he matched his pace to hers, then with a glance at his slim waterproof watch, he suggested, 'Perhaps you'd like a short rest and a pre-dinner drink?'

'That would be nice,' she agreed, and headed for the steps.

Matthew swam to the side and heaved himself out. By the time she'd reached the top of the steps he was waiting with a couple of white towelling robes.

She noted, with a feeling like butterflies in her stomach, that he had a strong, lithe, well-formed body, with broad shoulders and lean hips. His olive-toned skin was smooth and healthy-looking, with a sprinkle of crisp dark hair on his chest and legs.

They made their way to a poolside table, and as soon

as they were seated one of the bar staff came hurrying up.

'What would you like, Kate?' Matthew queried. Then, as she hesitated, 'A dry martini, perhaps?'

She shook her head. 'No, thank you. I like gin, but I *loathe* vermouth.'

'Then what about a gin and tonic?'

'Lovely.'

As they relaxed and sipped their drinks he remarked, his eyes on her bare left hand, 'I see you're not engaged?'.

'No.'

'Not even unofficially?'

She shook her head.

'A live-in lover, perhaps?'

'No.'

'Anyone with...shall we say...special claims?'

She hesitated, wondering whether to try and explain about Tony, then decided against it. 'No, not really.'

Without her realizing it, the last hour or so had dispelled all her doubts and uncertainties. She never had, and never would, feel this kind of excitement over Tony. No matter what happened between Matthew and herself, she knew now that she could never marry Tony, and she must tell him so as soon as possible.

Perhaps she could phone him?

But, no, Matthew had said the phones were down, and even if they hadn't been she couldn't break the news in that cowardly way. As soon as the roads were open she must carry on and see Tony, tell him to his face.

She felt sad for him and, though she had never made any promises, guilty that he was bound to be hurt.

'Another drink?' Matthew queried. 'Or would you prefer a final swim?' He sounded light-hearted and happy, as though her answer had been the one he'd hoped for.

Her mood soaring to match his, she shrugged off the towelling robe. 'The last one to reach the far end is a slowcoach.'

They hit the water together and came up doing a racing crawl. Kate had been her college champion, and, though Matthew beat her, the respect and admiration in his eyes warmed her.

After pacing each other for a few more lengths, he observed, 'It's almost seven-thirty. You must be ready to eat?'

When she nodded, he heaved himself out and turned to offer her a hand. His touch was like an electric shock.

As she stood by his side the top of her head was level with his chin. She glanced up at him. Drops of water trickled down his lean cheeks and beaded his thick, dark lashes. Before she could look away, his brilliant green-gold eyes met and held hers.

The magic was mutual. And for what seemed an age they stood quite still, gazing into each other's eyes as though under a spell.

It was Matthew who broke the silence to say huskily, 'The spa is full to capacity and the restaurants will be crowded, so shall we have dinner in my apartment?'

On the surface the question was a simple one, but even in her rapt state Kate realised that he was asking for a great deal more than her approval of where they ate.

Yet she never thought of saying no. It was so right. So inevitable.

Her own voice equally husky, she answered, 'Yes.' She knew with a surge of gladness that she could, without hesitation, give him what was in effect a commitment.

When she had finished dressing, and had pulled a comb through her hastily dried curls, Kate found

Matthew waiting for her, and they made their way back to his suite together.

It was dinnertime, and the wide corridors were full of people going to and from the various restaurants, and standing in groups discussing the inclement weather.

But to Kate and Matthew, who were in a little world of their own, it was as if no one else existed, and though they walked a decorous foot apart, no two lovers could have been closer.

From time to time they smiled at each other, smiles that said they had an understanding and shared a wonderful secret.

When they reached the privacy of his apartment, he turned her into his arms and kissed her gently, sealing their unspoken pledge.

The touch of his lips was as heady as any wine, and she would have been more than willing to stay in his embrace, but after one kiss he released her.

His air was relaxed and contented, as if he'd finally found what he'd been searching for. There was no need to rush or grab, his manner said. Having met and acknowledged a mutual response, an emotional commitment, they had all the time in the world to get to know and enjoy one another.

In a blissful daze she curled up on the settee and watched him draw the curtains to shut out the snowy night, before putting on some soft music.

The dinner he ordered came promptly, and they sat in front of a blazing log fire, picnic-fashion, with plates on their knees.

As they ate he asked casually, 'Who are the Wallaces? How did you come to be travelling with them?'

She told him, leaving out only her reason for going to New York. Then, with an uneasy feeling that amounted almost to guilt, she wondered if she should tell him everything.

But she couldn't bear the thought that it might spoil things between them. When he'd asked about boyfriends, she hadn't been strictly truthful. What if he was angry that she had lied, if only by omission?

As she hesitated, unwilling to mar this perfect happiness, he went on to talk about something else, and the moment was lost.

After they'd finished eating, Matthew switched off the lights and sat with his arm around her shoulders while they watched the flickering flames and listened to the love duet from *Madam Butterfly*.

When the beautiful emotional music faded into silence, as though it was the most natural thing in the world, he took her hand and led her to bed.

During her years at college, having to a great extent recovered her confidence, she'd had several boyfriends. But she had never taken a lover.

Nor had she been tempted to.

Now, though a complete innocent, she went willingly, eagerly, offering this man all she had to give.

For his part he brought to the act of love not only passion but something tender and special, caring, a concern for her feelings as a woman.

Afterwards, when he held her close and cradled her head on his shoulder, Kate knew she'd never been so happy in the whole of her life.

The following morning she awoke to the same feeling of joy and fulfilment, and when he held out his arms she went into them as if she belonged there.

After a late and leisurely breakfast they watched the weekend weather news on television, followed by an update on road conditions. The area report confirmed that it had stopped snowing and the wind had dropped.

Sounding regretful, Matthew said, 'As soon as the roads are clear I need to head for New York myself. I have an important Wall Street meeting scheduled for Monday...'

Then he added more cheerfully, 'But I doubt if anything will be moving just yet...'

When it became plain that he was right, nothing *was* moving and probably wouldn't be for another twenty-four hours, he smiled at her and said, 'As we have another day's grace, I suggest we make the most of it. Have you ever been on a skidoo?'

'No.'

'Well, believe me, it's fun.'

'I believe you,' she assured him.

'Want to try it?'

'I certainly do.'

Sounding jubilant, he invited, 'Then let's go.'

His declaration that skidooing was fun turned out to be an understatement, and she took to it like the proverbial duck takes to water.

Sitting behind him on the small but powerful snowmobile, she laughed aloud as they traversed forest tracks at what seemed to be breakneck speed.

Once they were out on the frozen lake, and the trees had ceased to flash past, their pace appeared more sedate.

After an idyllic day they returned late afternoon to sit cross-legged in front of the fire and toast English muffins, which they ate lathered in butter.

Licking her buttery fingers, Kate declared that the simple fare was more delicious than smoked salmon or caviare, and Matthew laughingly agreed.

But if the day had been wonderful the night was even more so, and it came as a shock when she awoke the next morning to find that she was alone in the big bed.

A note was propped up on the bedside cabinet. She read the hasty scrawl.

Kate, darling,
Leaving at first light to join the search for a missing
skier. When I get back we must talk.

                                                Matthew.

Wondering what he wanted to talk to her about, hoping she knew, she went to shower and dress. She had
just run a comb through her short blonde curls when
there was a knock at the door.

It was the same young man who had delivered her the
swimsuit. 'Morning, Miss Hunter. Mr Wallace asked me
to tell you that the main roads are clear and they will be
ready to start in about ten minutes.'

'Oh...' she said blankly. Then, trying to pull herself
together, 'Thank you. Please will you tell him I'll be
there directly?'

Not wanting to keep the Wallaces waiting, she threw
her belongings back in her case as quickly as possible,
and wrote a note to Matthew explaining that she had to
go. "...but I should be back in Adoga by Tuesday evening." She added, "Love, Kate" and her telephone
number.

It made her sad to leave without saying a proper goodbye, but the sooner she told Tony the truth the better.
Then, if what Matthew wanted to talk about was their
future together, she would be free to listen to whatever
he suggested with a totally clear conscience.

Snowploughs had been through and, though still hazardous, their route was comparatively clear. With only a
brief stop for lunch, they would have been in New York
City by early afternoon if fate hadn't decided to take a
hand.

Just outside the small village of Wilham the car gave
a couple of apologetic coughs, and a few hundred yards
further on stuttered to a stop.

It was Sunday and the only garage was closed.

Luckily there was a small motel nearby and, sighing at the vagaries of fortune, they booked in for the night.

The phones here were working, and while the Wallaces put a call through to their son Kate phoned Tony.

'There was a white-out further north, and I'm afraid we were snowbound.'

'I guessed as much.' He sounded upset and anxious.

When she told him they were delayed yet again, he got even more agitated. 'Tell me where you are and I'll come and fetch you.'

'No, really…' With the news she had to impart weighing down her spirits, that was the last thing she wanted. 'We'll be setting off again as soon as the car is fixed.'

'When will that be?'

'Probably tomorrow morning, so I'll see you some time in the afternoon.' Before he could argue, she said a hurried goodbye and replaced the receiver.

On Monday morning the local mechanic fitted a new fuel pump and they were on their way before lunchtime. Even so it was late afternoon before a yellow cab dropped Kate outside a fine old brownstone on East Sixty-fifth.

The maid had just opened the door and taken her case and outdoor things when Tony came hurrying into the hall, his thin dark face eager. 'Darling! I'd begun to think you'd never get here.'

He seized her hand and hurried her into a luxuriously furnished living-room, where a slight, elegant woman with grey hair and a patrician face was waiting with a warm smile, both hands outstretched.

As Kate was drawn into a welcoming embrace Tony said proudly, 'Mother, this is Kate.' He sounded like a small boy showing off a prize trophy.

Weighed down by the knowledge of why she was

here, Kate's greeting was somewhat stilted. 'How do you do, Mrs Newman?'

'My first husband's name was Newman; he died when Tony was just a year old, and I married Charles when Tony was three—' She broke off. 'But I'm rambling... What I wanted to say was, please don't be formal. Call me Grace.' With another hug, she added, 'I've been *so* looking forward to meeting Tony's fiancée, and when you and he are married, I do hope you'll call me Mother.'

As Kate turned reproachful eyes on Tony he said hurriedly, 'If you've been on the way since Friday you must be exhausted. Let me show you to your room so you can put your feet up before dinner.'

'How long can you stay?' Grace asked hopefully.

'I must go back first thing tomorrow,' Kate told her. 'I have to start work on Wednesday morning.'

'Oh, what a shame,' Grace sympathised. 'But it will make things so much easier when you move to New York. Tony said you were worried about finding a job and accommodation, but I'm sure my stepson can find you something for the time being. And you're more than welcome to stay here.'

'You're very kind,' Kate said in a strangled voice. 'But I—'

'Come on, darling.' Tony urged her towards the door. 'Let's get you settled in and we can talk later.'

Grace touched a bell by the mantelpiece. 'I'll ask Mary to bring a pot of tea up.'

'How *could* you?' Kate demanded as soon as the door of her room closed behind them. 'You've let your mother believe everything's settled when it's nothing of the kind.'

'But it could be,' he said eagerly. 'All you have to do is say yes.'

'I can't,' she told him flatly. 'I'm sorry—more sorry than I can say—but I can't marry you.'

'You don't mean it. You're just angry with me for jumping the gun.'

'Yes, I am angry with you,' she admitted. 'You've made things a great deal more difficult for everyone. But I *do* mean it. I know now that I don't love you in the way a wife should love her husband. I'm fond of you, but you must see that fondness isn't enough.'

'It is for me,' he argued stubbornly. 'I don't want a grand passion.'

'Well, I do,' Kate said simply.

He looked surprised, almost shocked. 'Don't be silly, darling. You're far too sensible and level-headed. If anyone looked like offering you passion on a grand scale, you'd run a mile.'

Clearly he'd taken the calm, dispassionate front she showed the world to be the real woman.

She bit her lip. If only he knew!

'I'm right, aren't I?' he pursued.

'It doesn't matter whether you're right or not. What does matter is that you accept the fact that I can't marry you and—'

There was a tap at the door.

'That will be Mary with your tea.' He failed to hide his relief. 'So I'll leave you to relax...'

Cool off, was what he meant.

'Dinner's at seven-thirty... Oh, and please, Kate, don't say anything tonight to upset Mother. You may feel differently by the morning.'

Before she could reply, he had opened the door for the young maid and made good his escape.

Worried and agitated, Kate drank her tea and wondered what to do for the best. She hated living a lie, even for a short time, and if his mother went on in the

same vein over dinner it would make things very difficult.

But would it help matters to blurt out the truth?

No, she couldn't do that. Though it was Tony's own
fault that the situation was so awkward, she owed him
some consideration.

Perhaps it would be best to say as little as possible
and leave him to give whatever explanation he thought
best after she'd gone?

Her case and things had been brought up, and, having
changed into a simple black cocktail dress, at a quarter
past seven Kate reluctantly went downstairs.

Tony greeted her with a show of enthusiasm, but she
saw his hazel eyes were wary.

'What will you have to drink, darling?'

'A dry sherry, please.'

Grace nodded her approval. 'Charles, my second husband, considered sherry a very civilised pre-dinner drink.

'Of course, being in the diplomatic service he travelled a great deal, and when we were first married we
spent a lot of time in England and on the continent.
Though there was quite a big age-gap between his son
and mine, both the boys—'

She broke off as the door opened. 'Ah, here's my
stepson now. Matt, dear, come and meet Tony's fiancée.'

Kate turned to find herself looking straight into
Matthew Carran's green-gold eyes.

The shock was severe, and mutual.

Matthew recovered first, but it was still several seconds before he took the hand she had automatically ex-
tended and said, 'How do you do, Miss...?'

'Hunter,' Tony supplied, while Kate stood mute and
frozen. 'Kate Hunter.'

'How do you do, Miss Hunter?'

'I'm sure there's no need to be so formal,' Grace

chided her stepson. 'Kate will soon be part of the family.'

Apparently becoming aware of the tension, she hurried on, 'The poor girl's had a terrible time getting here. First she and the couple she was travelling with were snowed up, then the car broke down and they had to spend last night in some dreary motel...'

There was no response, and so, looking somewhat helpless, she fell back on practicalities. 'Now, you've just time for a drink before dinner...'

'I'm dining out,' Matthew said abruptly. 'So if you'll excuse me, I must go and get changed.'

'What's eating him?' Tony asked of no one in particular as the door closed behind his stepbrother.

'Perhaps the meeting at the bank didn't go well,' Grace suggested. 'Though he doesn't usually let things like that bother him.'

Turning to Kate, she apologised. 'I'm sorry Matt was a little abrupt, dear. But please don't let it upset you.' Then, with concern, she said, 'You've gone deathly pale.'

The description was apt. Kate felt as if she'd been stabbed to the heart. Somehow she found her voice and said, 'I'm rather tired.'

'There's no wonder! And you've got another journey tomorrow, you poor thing. Well, as soon as we've eaten, you must have an early night.'

When the meal was served Kate ate what was put in front of her like an automaton, still in a state of shock, tasting nothing.

Though she made an attempt to act normally and join in the conversation, afterwards she had no idea what they'd talked about. Desperate to be alone, the only thought in her mind was to somehow hang on until she could escape to her room.

As soon as the coffee had been cleared away Grace,

clearly concerned about her, came to her aid. 'If you want to go straight up, my dear, please do. We can get to know each other and discuss your wedding plans next time you come.'

She gave Kate a hug. 'Now the ice is broken I hope you'll decide to stay with us when you move to the city. It would be so nice for you and Tony to be together... But as I say, we'll talk about it another time, when you're not so shattered. Goodnight, my dear.'

'Goodnight,' Kate answered in an impeded voice, 'and thank you. You're very kind.'

Apparently convinced she was still angry, Tony said a guarded, 'Goodnight, darling,' and kissed her cheek.

'Aren't you going to take Kate up?' his mother suggested.

'Really, there's no need,' Kate protested, and, with another hasty goodnight, fled.

Once in her room she sat on the bed, her whole being leaden with despair. How could fate have played such a cruel trick?

But it was her own stupidity in not telling Matthew the truth straight away that had made it possible. If she'd told him about Tony when he'd asked about boyfriends, none of this would have happened.

Now it was too late. He thought she and Tony were engaged and that she had deliberately cheated on her fiancé. In the instant they had looked straight at each other, she had seen the icy contempt and bitter condemnation in his eyes.

Moving like a very old woman, she showered and prepared for bed, then, finding no comfort, lay huddled beneath the duvet.

Though the bedroom was centrally heated, she shivered, gripped by a bone-deep cold, a desolation too bleak even for tears.

The blessed oblivion of sleep refused to come, and

she was still lying wide awake staring blindly into the darkness when the door opened and closed quietly.

'Who's there?' Sitting bolt-upright, she fumbled for the switch on the bedside lamp.

Before she could find it the light flashed on. Blinking in the sudden brightness, she saw Matthew standing with his back to the door panels. He was still wearing an evening jacket and bow tie, but in spite of the civilised garb he looked dangerous, white-lipped and quietly furious.

He came to sit on the edge of the bed, and she caught her breath in sudden fear. 'There's no need to look so scared,' he told her with withering scorn. 'Now I know just what sort of woman you are I wouldn't soil my hands on you.'

'Please, Matthew, listen to me—'

'So who did you sleep with last night?'

She flinched. 'I don't blame you for thinking the worst. I'm sorry—'

'Not half as sorry as I am,' he broke in savagely. 'You're a wonderful actress, Kate. You fooled me completely with that air of sweet innocence. I actually thought I'd found the kind of woman I'd been looking for...'

His green eyes cold as any glacier, he added deliberately, 'It came as quite a shock to discover you were nothing but a tramp.'

'I'm no such thing!' she choked.

'What else would you call a woman who jumps into bed with a man she's only just met whilst she's on her way to visit her fiancé?'

'But it wasn't like that! If you'd let me explain—'

'I didn't come to listen to any excuses. I came to make one thing quite clear. You will not marry Tony.'

'I've already told him I can't marry him.'

'I'm pleased to know you've still got some scrap of

decency left. Or was it simply that your cover had been blown?'

'I told him before I ever realised you two were related.' Desperately she went on. 'He'd asked me repeatedly to marry him, or at least get engaged, but I'd never said I would. When he begged me to come to New York to meet his mother I agreed, but I made it clear that didn't mean the answer was yes... I still hadn't made up my mind. After I'd met you, I knew I couldn't marry him. I told him so as soon as I arrived.'

'Then why did Grace introduce you as his fiancée?'

With a suffocating feeling of hopelessness, Kate tried to explain. 'Because, in spite of what I'd said, he'd let her think we *were* engaged. When I realised, I was angry with him. But he asked me not to say anything to upset her... I think he was hoping I'd change my mind.'

It didn't need Matthew's cynical expression to tell her that he didn't believe a word.

Softly, lethally, he said, 'I want you out of my house first thing in the morning. I never want to have to set eyes on you again. And from now on leave Tony alone. If you don't, I'll be forced to tell him everything that happened between us.

'Oh, and a further word of warning. I hold the purse-strings. If you were hoping to marry into money, forget it. Neither Grace nor Tony have any of their own; he's dependent on me for a home and a job...'

No wonder Tony had at times seemed to resent his brother, Kate thought dully.

'He's just got into his stride at Carran Enterprises,' Matthew added deliberately, 'and I'd hate to have to dismiss him.'

Turning his back, he walked away, and a moment later the door closed behind him.

Knowing she couldn't stay here a minute longer than she had to, Kate struggled out of bed. Sobbing under her breath, dry, harsh sobs that hurt her throat and chest, she threw on her clothes and repacked her case as fast as she could.

Then, tearing a page from her diary, she scrawled a note.

Dear Tony,

It really is all over between us. You have to believe that I can't marry you, and remember that I never said I would.

I'm sincerely sorry if I've hurt either you or your mother. Please don't try to get in touch. Just leave me alone.

Kate

When she'd propped the jagged piece of paper against the lamp, she pulled on her outdoor things, turned off the light and, her case bumping against her leg, crept down the stairs.

In the faint, greenish glow from the hall security light she slid back the bolts on the heavy front door, hands trembling, and let herself out into the bitterly cold night.

As she reached the bottom of the wide steps a cab that had just dropped off some late-night revellers came cruising past.

Even before she lifted her hand the driver had spotted her and was drawing to a halt. She stumbled in, shaking in every limb.

Looking over his shoulder, he queried, 'You sick or something?'

'Just cold.'

He shrugged. 'Where to?'

Reaction had set in, and her teeth were chattering so much she could hardly say the words. 'Please will you take me to the nearest inexpensive hotel?'

CHAPTER FIVE

THE next morning, Kate returned to Adoga and tried to pick up the threads of her life.

Each day she got up, showered and dressed, did her work with her customary efficiency, ate her meals, talked to people and even smiled.

But all the time she felt dead, as if her life force had been extinguished and only will-power was producing this parody of living.

As the weeks crawled past, instead of starting to feel better she lost her appetite, and had difficulty keeping down what little she did manage to eat. Certain smells made her nauseous, and she couldn't face either tea or coffee.

A couple of times she had been forced to leave an administrative meeting and hurry to the Ladies' Room to wait, grey-faced and trembling, until the sickness had passed.

On the third occasion, when she returned to the admin room Mrs Wallace, her eyes sharp with suspicion and disapproval, asked pointedly, 'Still feeling ill, Miss Hunter? What do you think it could be?'

'Some kind of gastric flu, I imagine.' Kate tried to keep her voice steady.

'It's lasting an awful long time. I should visit a doctor if I were you.' Then she added a shade maliciously, 'I notice your boyfriend hasn't been up lately.'

'No.'

Kate left it at that, preferring not to think about Tony.

Rather than answering her plea to leave her alone, he had written and phoned repeatedly. She had torn up his letters unopened, and, after putting down the phone every time she heard his voice, had finally, in desperation, asked that no calls should be put through to her.

Her sickness continued, and the following weekend her pregnancy test proved positive. Seeing it had come as a shock to her, the elderly doctor asked, 'You have no…er…partner?'

'No,' she answered flatly.

'But you do know who the father is?'

'Yes.'

'So he'll be able to help you?'

'I have no intention of asking him.'

'It isn't easy to bring up a child when you're alone, and there are other options, you know. You might want to consider adoption?'

'No. I'll manage somehow.'

It was Matthew's baby and she wanted to keep it.

For the first time in weeks a trickle of warmth began to disperse some of the cold greyness that had shrouded her spirit.

That afternoon she sat in her room and tried to think what to do for the best. If her sickness continued, it would be impossible to hide the fact that she was pregnant.

Mrs Wallace had already guessed.

Kate sighed. The immediate future looked bleak. She had very little money, and it would be difficult to carry on with her job when her condition became more pronounced. She had noticed that Mrs Wallace didn't take kindly to pregnant staff, judging by the way she'd treated 'offending' members in the past.

It might be best if she moved back to New York. Surely she could get a room and a job of some kind?

But what would she do when she could no longer work? How could she provide a home for her child?

Trying not to despair, she was mentally exploring

every avenue when there was a knock at the door. Before she could reach it it opened and Tony walked in.

He looked thin and gaunt, his face tense. Clearly the situation had hit him hard. 'Please, Kate, I *have* to talk to you.' He sounded close to tears.

'It isn't any good,' she said wearily. 'No amount of talking will alter the fact that it's all over between us. I can't marry you.'

'Because you don't love me?'

'No one can love to order.'

'You said you were fond of me.'

'I am. But fondness isn't enough.'

'It's all I'm asking. I don't want passionate love.'

'Look, even if I did love you, there's no way I could marry you.'

'Give me one good reason why not.'

At breaking point, she said, 'Because I'm expecting another man's child.' She saw him blink as he absorbed the shock. 'You'd better sit down,' she said tonelessly.

He sank into the nearest chair and put his head in his hands. After a moment he asked in a muffled voice, 'Who is this man?'

'I've no intention of telling you.'

'Do you love him?'

'Yes.'

'Are you going to marry him?'

'No.'

'Why not?'

'He wouldn't want to marry me.'

Tony lifted his head and asked, 'Have you told him about the baby?'

'No.'

'But you are going to?'

'No. Everything's over between us. It was just a...a brief madness.'

He gave a kind of sigh. 'Are you intending to go ahead and have the baby?'

'Of course I'm going to have it.'

'How are you planning to support it?'

'I don't know,' she admitted. 'But I'll think of something.'

When he said nothing, she added, 'I know it must have come as a blow, and it must seem—'

'It seems like a miracle,' he broke in, his face suddenly eager. 'The answer to my prayers. Kate, please marry me, and I promise I'll never mention this man again. We'll tell everyone the baby's mine. I'll take care of both of you. We'll be a family...'

Wondering why on earth he was prepared to take on another man's child, she shook her head. 'No—no, I couldn't. You'd only regret it afterwards.'

'I wouldn't regret it.'

'You can say that now, but suppose when it was too late you changed your mind? It just isn't fair to you.'

'But I want to.' Urgently he added, 'If only you'd agree to marry me it would solve so many problems— be the best thing for all our sakes. I *need* you, Kate.'

'For the last time, there are reasons that make it quite *impossible* for me to marry you.'

Perhaps he heard the ring of finality in her voice as the death knell of his hopes.

Suddenly he was on his knees by her side, clasping her hands, his anguish and despair evident. 'Please, just listen to me. I'm going to tell you something I've never told another living soul...'

They were married a fortnight later in a quiet, civil ceremony with only Tony's mother, his cousin Derek—who had made a flying visit from Canada to be best man— and the necessary witnesses present.

Delighted to hear that their wedding was to be so

soon, Grace had proved to be kindness itself, helping
Kate to find a cheap hotel room and a temporary job as
a dental receptionist when she left Adoga for New York.

Tony hadn't mentioned their estrangement, and if his
mother thought it peculiar that Kate had gone so early
on that morning, without even saying goodbye, she kept
it to herself.

Prepared for the worst, Kate had been relieved to find
that, perhaps for his stepmother's sake, Matthew had
played it cool. Though making his opposition to the marriage plain, he had given no specific reason, nor had he
deprived Tony of his job.

She had been even more relieved that he'd made it
his business to be on the other side of the world when
the wedding took place.

Both Tony and his mother had tried hard to persuade
Kate to move into Matthew's house, but she had refused
point-blank to even set foot inside.

'I know that for some reason you and Big Brother
didn't hit it off,' Tony had said, 'but honestly, darling,
you wouldn't have to see that much of him.' Then he'd
added practically, 'And it would be terribly expensive to
get anything else halfway decent.'

'I want us to have a place of our own. I don't care if
it is shabby, and I'm willing to work for as long as I
can to help pay the rent.'

Looking worried, he'd protested, 'But I don't like the
idea of you having to work—especially in your present
condition. And I want you and our baby to have somewhere nice to live...'

When all his arguments failed to move her, they had
set about looking for some accommodation they could
afford.

A couple of days before the wedding they'd found a
dingy furnished apartment on the top floor of a tenement

block near the Hudson River, and they moved in as soon as they were married.

When her temporary job ended, Kate managed to find work as a waitress in a backstreet diner. The hours were long, the pay poor, and she was on her feet all day.

Anxious on her behalf, Tony begged her to give it up.

Shaking her head, she said simply, 'We need the money.'

'I can't bear to think of you slaving like this when you ought to be resting... Look, let me talk to Big Brother. He isn't an ogre, and if he knew how things were I'm sure he'd—'

'If you ask your stepbrother for help I'll walk out and never come back.'

Her quiet threat was enough to silence him.

Waiting on tables was exhausting, and Kate was permanently tired. But she was only too glad that the debilitating sickness had passed, and she counted her blessings and made light of it.

True to his word, Tony never once mentioned the baby's true father. He always acted as if the child was his, and, like an excited small boy with a special gift to give, he was dying to tell his mother the good news.

Her heart in her mouth, Kate extracted a promise that he'd wait at least two months, and then, when the time came for the child to be born, he would simply say that it had been a seven-month pregnancy.

Knowing how he felt about her, the last thing she wanted was for Matthew to have the faintest suspicion that the baby might be his.

On her side, the love that had sprung into being at their first meeting had never wavered, and she cherished the life growing inside her—not only for its own sake, but because it was a part of him.

She thought often of their brief time together, and like

a smashed mirror the pieces gleamed brilliant and razor-sharp.

But sometimes in her dreams she felt again a sweet, singing happiness, the delight of being held close to his heart...

'Take care not to scald yourself,' Matthew's voice instructed. 'It's very hot.'

For a second or two the memory of those dreams stayed with her, and she remained trapped in the past, gazing up at him, her eyes far away, soft and enormous.

Then, abruptly released into the present, she found herself back in a snowbound house, sitting in front of a blazing stove while Matthew stood over her with a steaming mug of hot tea.

'Thank you.' She took it awkwardly and, despite his warning, almost succeeded in spilling it.

A strange note in his voice, he remarked, 'Just for that instant you looked radiantly happy. What were you thinking about?'

'N-nothing in particular,' she stammered.

He seemed about to probe further then, changing his mind, he turned away abruptly and, pulling another chair closer to the stove, picked up his own mug.

Though she carefully avoided looking in his direction while she drank her tea, Caroline was only too aware that his eyes never for an instant left her face, and she wondered if it was his intention to fluster and intimidate her.

Well, if it was, he was succeeding.

Made more than uneasy by that deliberate scrutiny, she moved restlessly, once again gripped by an alarming sensation of being trapped.

If only they'd gone down before the conditions got so bad... Matthew knew the mountain and the weather patterns well, so how had he come to misread the signs and make such a mistake?

But what if it hadn't been a mistake? What if it had been deliberate, planned?

Perhaps he had insisted on going on to Prospect Point *knowing* the weather would close in, *intending* them to be trapped here alone.

The thought brought a suffocating panic.

Gripping the mug until her knuckles showed white, she did her best to fight it down, aware that giving way to it might only precipitate a confrontation she feared.

'You seem nervous,' he remarked mockingly. 'Is it because you're alone here with me?'

'No, I'm not nervous.'

'Liar,' he jeered softly.

'What makes you say that?'

'Well, you're either a liar or a fool, and I don't believe you're a fool.'

Lifting her chin, she asked, 'Do you mean I have grounds for being nervous?'

'You may well have.'

The quiet words made a cold shiver run through her. Taking a deep breath, she said as steadily as possible, 'I think you're just trying to scare me.'

His face sardonic above the dark polo-necked sweater, he queried, 'Why should I want to do that?'

'Because you don't like me.'

'Do you think not liking you is a good enough reason?'

'Is there any other?'

'Perhaps I enjoy seeing you look at me with big, apprehensive eyes, like you're doing now.'

Without stopping to think, she accused, 'You've developed a sadistic streak.'

'*Developed*... Then you don't think I've always had one?'

'I've no idea,' she said jerkily. 'You may have been the kind of cruel little boy who enjoyed inflicting pain on anything weaker than himself.'

He shook his head. 'You were right the first time. The desire to hurt is comparatively recent, and it's directed against...'

She saw the gleam in his green eyes, and shuddered uncontrollably.

'But maybe you would like to guess?'

He was amusing himself, she knew. Yet she had to play his game, she couldn't afford not to. Swallowing hard, she said, 'Women?'

'One woman in particular.'

Without much hope, she suggested, 'Your ex-fiancée?'

His well-cut lips twisted. 'Sara was too innocuous to arouse such strong feelings. No, I was thinking of a woman I met at Clear Lake. A woman called Kate.

'She wasn't particularly beautiful, rather fascinating and intriguing. She seemed to have a rare warmth and innocence, a kind of inner glow.'

His voice harsh, he went on, 'But the air of innocence was as false as she was. She turned out to be little more than a tramp. Have you any idea what it's like to think you've found perfection and then be totally disillusioned...?'

Caroline felt raw, flayed by his bitterness.

'Yet I couldn't get her out of my mind. The thought of her haunted me. I couldn't work, I couldn't eat, I couldn't sleep. It was a kind of madness.

'When I met Sara and we got engaged, I told myself I was on the way to being cured. But soon, with a woman's intuition, she guessed there was someone else.

'Though I never told her who, and made it quite plain that the whole thing was over and done with, she didn't believe me. That was the real reason she finally ended our engagement. She thought I was still obsessed...

'And she was right. Even after all this time Kate's like a disease in my blood, a recurring fever that I have no immunity to.

'And though you look nothing like her, for some strange reason you remind me of her.'

Her chest feeling as though it was constricted by iron bands, Caroline sat still and frozen.

He stood up, and with lean fingers gripping her upper arms drew her to her feet, his eyes holding hers. 'Perhaps that's why I kissed you the other night. Why I said I might not be able to keep my hands off you.'

His voice husky, he added, 'And now we're alone together, I find I can't.'

Last night it had been an enchantment of light and sweetness. This time the sorcery was dark and bitter. But the spell was equally powerful.

She had wanted his love then and she wanted it now, the yearning made more intense by the empty years that had stretched between.

Only it wasn't love he felt, she reminded herself desperately, just an obsession he was unable to free himself from.

He bent his head to kiss her. She turned sharply away and his lips grazed her cheek.

'Leave me alone,' she whispered, her hands lifting to ward him off.

'There's no need to look quite so frightened,' he said caustically. 'After all, you're no shrinking virgin. You have been married.'

'That has nothing to do with it. I don't want to take the place of a ghost from the past. I'd find it degrading to be made love to simply because I remind you of...of someone else.'

'You're a flesh and blood woman, no substitute, and

if it would make you any happier I promise to say your name while I'm making love to you—'

'I don't want you to touch me,' she broke in agitatedly.

'You don't mean that.' One hand deftly removed the pins from her hair while the other cupped her chin and lifted her face to his.

'Please don't...' The protest was silenced as his lips teased hers with featherlight kisses before lingering tantalisingly at the corner of her mouth.

Every nerve in her body sang into life, and, terrified by her own reaction, she choked, 'I mean it! I don't want you to make love to me.'

'That's a lie,' he returned softly. 'The first time I kissed you I could have taken you to bed. In that you're very like Kate.'

She closed her eyes against the pain.

His hands slipped under her cream wool sweater. While one spread across the small of her back and held her to him the other found the slight curve of her breast and through the thin material of her bra caressed the firm, waiting nipple.

His cheek against hers, he said huskily, 'You *do* want me to make love to you. Don't you?'

She wanted to say no, she *had* to say no, but she loved him so much—if the word 'love' could adequately express this deep emotional commitment—and her tongue refused to frame the lie.

While she struggled to make it his mouth covered hers, coaxing her lips to part for him, and when he deepened the kiss she was lost, all hope of saving herself gone.

He kissed her like a man who had hungered for her a long, lonely while.

The awareness of his need fanned hers into a flame

that threatened to engulf her, and she began to tremble violently.

Feeling that betraying movement, he left her for a moment to switch off the light, then he laid her down on the thick mat in front of the stove and undressed her in the glow from the fire.

While it turned her creamy skin to rose he stripped off his own things and stretched out beside her, propping himself on one elbow.

As he did so a log settled with a flare and a shower of bright sparks, lighting his dark face, turning it into a devil mask.

Suddenly, shockingly, she was afraid of him. He could be cruel. *Had* been cruel. He'd said she reminded him of Kate, and he hated Kate, had confessed to a desire to hurt her...

She made a sound, a moan so soft it could be heard beneath the noise of the blizzard still raging outside.

He looked down at her sharply and read the very real fear in her face. 'Don't look like that,' he said harshly.

'I—I can't help it,' she whispered.

Putting out a hand, he brushed a strand of silky brown hair away from her cheek. The gesture held something of tenderness. 'There's no need to be afraid. I won't hurt you, or do anything you don't want me to do.'

In spite of everything, she believed him, and as he began to kiss and caress her she relaxed, the gentle warmth of his touch filling her with a long-remembered pleasure.

She yearned to touch him in return, to slide her hands over his broad shoulders and run her fingers into the sprinkling of crisp dark hair that spread across his muscular chest, but, afraid of giving herself away, she lay quite still.

While his hands stroked and fondled her his lips

traced a scorching path from the smooth skin of her shoulder to her breast, and lingered there.

Though he was making love to her as though he had all the time in the world, she could sense the almost desperate urgency he was holding in check.

He had never pretended to even like her, let alone care anything for her feelings, and she was half expecting him to take her and satisfy his own needs without concerning himself too much about hers.

But with patience and skill he brought her to a pitch of wanting that had her body welcoming his with eagerness and delight.

As he lowered himself into the cradle of her hips she put her arms around his neck and buried her face against his throat.

As though sensing her total responsiveness, he made love to her then with a power and passion that carried them both through a storm of feeling and left them lying in each other's arms, spent and peaceful.

After a little while he peered down into her face and remarked, 'You're a woman of eloquent silences... What are you thinking, Caroline?'

She had been remembering how he had promised to say her name while he was making love to her. And he had. But the name that he'd groaned at the height of his passion had been Kate.

Not wanting to remind him, she half shook her head.

'If you won't tell me your thoughts, tell me what you're feeling?'

He'd cared enough about her to make sure he more than fulfilled her needs, and her body was in a state of blissful satisfaction. Without thinking, she answered simply, 'Surprised and grateful.'

'Good God, woman,' he burst out. 'Did you imagine I was the kind of selfish brute who'd only consider his own pleasure?'

'Not if you'd been making love to someone you…you cared about… But I—I thought you just wanted to use me.'

'Yet you didn't fight to stop me.'

'I couldn't stop you,' she protested. 'I tried to fight…you know I did.'

'But you were fighting yourself more than me. You could have stopped me with a single no if you'd really meant it.'

When she said nothing, silently acknowledging that that was almost certainly the truth, he asked, 'How long is it since you lost your husband?'

Shaken and alarmed by the question, she answered vaguely, 'More than two years.'

'Have you had a lover since?'

'No.'

'Why not? You're a young woman with natural needs and instincts.'

Her voice muffled, she said, 'I've never met anyone that I cared about.'

'Are you saying you'd only go to bed with someone you cared for?'

Realising too late where his interrogation was leading, she stammered, 'W-well, no…not exactly. What I meant was, I've never been *attracted* by anyone else.'

'Until now?'

Allowing for what had gone before, it was a reasonable conclusion to draw.

When she said nothing, he pursued. 'You must have loved your husband a great deal?'

Instead of simply saying yes, she spoke the truth. 'I was very fond of him.'

'Fond?' Matthew raised a sardonic brow. 'Somehow that hardly seems enough.'

'It was enough for him.'

Matthew smiled mirthlessly. 'I doubt if I'd be flattered to be told any woman was "fond" of me.'

'I don't think you've any need to worry.'

Almost instantly she regretted the hasty words. Oh, why couldn't she guard her unruly tongue instead of letting Matthew provoke her?

Rather to her surprise, he laughed. 'It's nice to know you still have some spirit. At first you appeared thin and pale and defeated, as though life had battered you into submission, but over the last month you've put on a little weight and lost that look of desolation.

'Tell me, Caroline, are you happy working for me?'

There was something in his voice that made her wary. 'I enjoy taking care of Caitlin,' she answered guardedly.

'What would you do if for some reason you had to leave?'

'I'd find another job.' She spoke levelly, though the very thought chilled her.

Noticing the faint shiver that ran through her, he said abruptly, 'The fire's burning low. You'd better get dressed.'

Suddenly awkward, embarrassed by her nakedness, she hurriedly collected her clothes and, head bent, began to pull them on.

Though she couldn't regret seizing that brief chance of bliss, now the euphoria was fading she was starting to feel uneasy, to question the wisdom of what she'd done.

But she had burnt her bridges and there was no going back.

When, finally, she glanced up, she saw that he, too, was fully dressed. He looked preoccupied, his expression bleak, as though his thoughts gave him no pleasure as he proceeded to throw logs into the stove. That done, he turned on the lights before enquiring, 'Are you hungry yet? There's plenty of canned food.'

She wasn't hungry, but, needing something to occupy her, she asked, 'Would you like me to start preparing a meal?'

Matthew shook his head. 'You got supper last night, and I'm quite skilled with a can-opener.' His eyes on her pale face, he added, 'I suggest you relax by the fire while I heat up some hash.'

Though his words showed consideration, they held not the slightest trace of warmth. Biting her lip, she sat down once more.

Aware that his gaze was still fixed on her, she tried not to look at him, but his will dragged her glance upwards.

Perhaps he saw the glitter of unshed tears, because he asked shortly, 'Regretting it?'

About to say no, she hesitated, then answered his question with a question of her own. 'Should I be?'

'Perhaps we both should.'

The secret hope she'd cherished—that the delight they had shared might make him soften towards her—shrivelled and died. He had sounded as if he disliked and despised both her and himself.

But it had been idiotic to hope that his feelings might change. She had known from the start that he didn't like her, and on his own admission he only wanted her because she reminded him of a woman he hated but was still obsessed by.

It seemed she was fated to be a two-way loser.

She was tired and emotionally exhausted, her spirits weighed down by a leaden despair. By the time he put the meal on the table she felt almost too weary to sit upright.

'I don't really want anything,' she mumbled. 'I'd rather go straight to bed.'

'You ought to eat first. I noticed you didn't have much at lunchtime. There's no heating apart from the stove, and if your blood sugar level drops too low, you'll feel cold in the night.'

With no strength to argue, she picked up her fork and made an effort to force down some of the tinned hash, which was surprisingly good.

They ate in silence, the only sounds the crackle and flare of the logs and the howling of the blizzard as it continued to fling snow against the windows.

By the time Caroline's plate was half empty she was drooping visibly, despite all her efforts.

'You'd better get some sleep,' he said curtly. 'I'll show you the only habitable bedroom. I've put a couple of extra blankets on the beds, so I hope you'll be warm enough...'

She followed him across the hall and into a nicely furnished room with twin beds.

'There's an *en suite* bathroom, but no hot water, I'm afraid.'

'Are you...?' She hesitated.

'I'll be along when I've cleared away and built up the stove for the night.'

After a quick wash in the unheated water, she took off her trousers and sweater and, leaving her under-clothes on, climbed into bed and pulled the covers over her.

She felt absolutely bone-weary, but, chilled from her visit to the bathroom, her feet like ice, she was unable to sleep.

Some half an hour later, when Matthew came to bed, she was still lying huddled beneath the blankets, wide awake and trying not to shiver.

As though her silent misery was a cry he heard, he asked, 'Not asleep?' She couldn't see his face in the darkness but his voice sounded concerned.

'No.'

'Why not?'

'I'm not very warm.'

She heard the faint creak of the mattress before he said, 'You'd better come in with me.'

When, surprised, she made no move, he added bitingly, 'Don't worry, I've no further designs on you. It's just that it will be much warmer if we share a bed.' Then he said impatiently, 'Well, are you coming or not?'

Unable to find sufficient strength to refuse the comfort he was offering, she whispered, 'Yes, please.'

Crossing the bare floor between the two beds, she crept in beside him, taking care not to touch him.

Reaching out an exploring hand, he muttered, 'No wonder you couldn't sleep; you're like ice.'

Drawing her against the warmth of his naked body, he settled her head on his chest, so that his chin rested on her hair, and said, 'Now try to relax.'

Enfolded in his arms, the strong beat of his heart beneath her cheek, she felt her misery replaced by a deep contentment, a happiness marred only by a loving concern for Caitlin.

But there was no need to worry, she tried to reassure herself. Matthew, who clearly loved the child he still believed to be his stepbrother's, had made sure she would be well cared for in their absence.

Mentally sending their daughter a goodnight hug and a kiss, Caroline prayed she was safely asleep and not missing them.

Matthew continued to hold her, and within a very short time she was comfortably warm. And though she wanted to prolong the pleasure of lying in his arms, in less than a minute she had drifted into sleep.

CHAPTER SIX

CAROLINE stirred and awoke to find it was almost daylight and she was alone in the bed. Sitting up, she peered through the window to find the snow had stopped and the morning showed signs of being a bright one.

After a hurried wash she borrowed a comb, pulled on her clothes and made her way to the kitchen, to be greeted by the appetising aroma of coffee.

Matthew was fully dressed and standing by the cooker, making what appeared to be coaster-size buckwheat pancakes.

Turning his head, he remarked, 'As you can see, the blizzard blew itself out overnight, and the snowplough's been through, so as soon as we've eaten we can start back.'

'Yes, I'd like to go as soon as possible in case Caitlin—'

'Caitlin will be fine,' he broke in, adding with a little edge to his voice, 'You sound concerned enough to be her mother rather than just her nanny.'

It seemed his mood had swung back to wanting to hurt rather than comfort.

'As her nanny, I'm *paid* to be concerned.'

'You're paid to give satisfaction—*job-wise*, that is. Though last night you were eminently successful in other fields,' he added sardonically, and watched the heated colour rise into her cheeks.

Biting her tongue, she held in check the angry retort she wanted to make. It would do no good to start a fight. With a quick wit and better self-control he was bound to win.

Turning the puffy golden pancakes onto two plates, he informed her, 'Breakfast is ready when you are.'

After one reproachful glance, she silently took her place at the table. Her ash-brown hair tumbled in a silky mass around her shoulders, and her oval face was still tinged with transient colour. Watching her pour thick, gooey maple syrup over her pancakes, Matthew thought, almost with surprise, how beautiful she was.

Her almond-shaped eyes were a clear aquamarine, with very long lashes. As she looked down those lashes seemed almost to brush her high cheekbones.

With her flawless, nearly translucent skin, she put him in mind of some pale and delicate watercolour, yet her mouth and chin showed both character and strength.

Glancing up incautiously, she met his eyes, and the colour in her cheeks deepened.

'You look quite different with your hair down,' he remarked evenly. 'Leave it that way; I prefer it.'

She would sooner have kept the rather staid image the bun gave her, but she said nothing, unwilling to argue.

They ate the rest of their breakfast without speaking, and when Caroline had cleared the table, Matthew helped her into her coat and they went out into the glistening white world.

As he closed the door behind them she caught her breath in a sigh. So much had happened since he'd first opened it. So much that could neither be forgotten nor undone, that had irrevocably altered their relationship.

Though not in a way she could feel either pleased or confident about. All he'd wanted was to use her as a kind of vaccine—to give him some immunity to what he'd described as a fever in his blood...

As she climbed into the car an even worse thought struck her. What if her surrender had jeopardised her job? Suppose, regretting what had happened, Matthew decided she was an embarrassment and made up his mind to get rid of her? He held the whip-hand, and there would be little, if anything, she could do...

The virgin snow, crisp and unsullied, shushed beneath their tyres as Matthew drove carefully along the drive and down to the main road. As he had mentioned earlier, the snowplough had been through and the Parkway was virtually clear.

Nature seemed intent on making up for the previous day's bad weather, and it was a glorious morning. Sun shone from a sky of Mediterranean blue and the very air sparkled, but, enveloped in a cold sweat of fear, Caroline failed to appreciate any of it.

When they reached the chalet Caitlin came running to meet them, and, throwing her arms around Caroline's knees, lifted her face to be kissed.

Stooping, trying to hide her emotion, Caroline gave the child a hug and a kiss.

'Hello, poppet, have you been having fun?' Matthew swung her up and, growling, pretended to nibble her ear, making her shriek with laughter.

When he put her down she trotted away to seize the hand of a pleasant-looking middle-aged woman and drag her over to Caroline. 'This is Gladys.'

Over the child's head the two women smiled at each other with perfect understanding.

'Everything all right?' Matthew asked.

'Fine,' Gladys answered cheerfully. 'When I put her to bed she asked where you both were, but was quite content when I assured her you'd be home this morning...'

Recalling her earlier suspicions that Matthew might have engineered their overnight stay, Caroline shot him a quick glance, but his face was bland, showing no trace of guilt or awareness.

'She told me Caro always tells her a toad story,'

Gladys went on. 'But when I didn't know one, she settled for the adventures of a dragon called Donald—'

'Can we go now?' Caitlin piped up, tugging at Gladys's skirt.

'She's impatient to join the other children,' the nanny explained. 'But I said we'd better stay here until you got back.'

'Can we go, Daddy?'

'Yes, you can go,' he answered.

Caitlin took Caroline's hand and raised an eager face. 'Would you like to come with us?'

'Yes, I'd—'

'No, not today,' Matthew broke in firmly. 'Caroline has things to do.'

Then he turned to Gladys, 'There's no shortage of staff, is there?'

'Oh, no, we've plenty of staff, and a full day planned,' Gladys said enthusiastically. 'All the young ones love their painting lessons, and the tumble gym is set up...'

'It's lots of fun,' Caitlin agreed.

'Then after lunch we're going on the toy train for a journey through Toyland and tea with Santa Claus.'

'And his elves and his reindeers...' Caitlin added happily, while the pair donned their outdoor things.

'Will you be putting her to bed yourselves tonight?' Gladys queried, when they were ready to go.

Flustered by the fact that Gladys seemed to regard them as a couple, rather than employer and employee, and wondering why Matthew had made no attempt to correct that assumption, Caroline said hastily, 'Yes, of course.'

'Then I'll bring her back here by six-thirty.'

'No need,' Matthew said. 'I'll come over and fetch her myself.'

After another hug and kiss, and a brief pause to collect Barnaby Bear, Gladys said, 'Come on, then, honey,' and, hand in hand, the pair set off for the main complex, Barnaby dangling by his striped scarf.

Deprived of her chance to settle once more into the role of nanny, and uneasy at being left alone with Matthew yet again, Caroline remarked a shade wildly, 'It seems as if your nursery programme is a great success.'

'As I said before, while it teaches and entertains the very young, it gives parents and nannies a chance to do their own thing... And the thing I'd like to do right now is take a hot shower. How about you?'

'That sounds wonderful.'

'Then, as this is a holiday, I thought we'd go out.'

'Go out?' she echoed.

'Surely you don't want to stay indoors on such a lovely day?'

'Well, no, but I—I'm Caitlin's nanny, a paid employee, and...' She faltered to a halt.

'After last night, isn't it a bit late to start worrying about that?'

All her earlier fears came rushing back. Hurriedly she said, 'I know you're regretting it, and I agree that it should never have happened, but I'm more than willing to put it behind me and forget about it if you—'

'*Can* you forget about it?'

'Yes, I can,' she lied hardily. 'I think it would be better for everyone if we returned to being just...just...'

'Employer and employee?' he queried, when she hesitated.

'Yes.'

'So you want to keep on working for me?' His green-gold eyes held a mocking gleam. 'You've no plans to leave?'

Unable to trust her voice, she shook her head.

'Well, if you wish to remain in my employment, all you have to remember is that you're being paid to do what I want you to do. Within reason,' he added sardonically. 'In other words, if I ask for your company as, say, a holiday companion, I expect to get it...'

Damn him! Caroline thought furiously. If it wasn't for Caitlin she wouldn't put up with his arrogance.

'Is that clear?'

After a moment she answered stiffly, 'Quite clear.'

He gave a little nod. Then, his tone milder now, he remarked, 'As we won't be doing anything strenuous, I suggest you wrap up well... And leave your hair down.' With a glinting smile that showed he knew her feelings exactly, he added, 'Please.'

Her thoughts in chaos, Caroline went to shower and change her clothes.

While she was still convinced it would have been safer to have got back to their old footing, she couldn't control a surge of excitement. An excitement that was laced with uncertainty, apprehension, a lingering anger and bewilderment.

If it was simply companionship he wanted, there must surely be some unattached women in a complex this size? Beautiful, sophisticated women, who would no doubt be only too pleased to gain the attention of a man as attractive as Matthew.

So why had he insisted on having *her* company, when he didn't even like her?

Whatever his motive, he'd made it quite plain that he was calling the tune, and she had no choice but to dance to it.

When she went back to the living-room he was ready and waiting, dressed in a sheepskin coat, his dark head bare.

He looked with disfavour at her hip-length jacket. 'Is that the warmest thing you have?'

'Yes,' she answered flatly.

With a slight shrug he led the way outside, where, to her surprise, there was a horse-drawn sleigh waiting.

The youth standing by the horse's head handed over the reins.

'Thanks.'

Matthew helped Caroline into the vehicle and when she was settled got in beside her. Though the sun still shone brightly, the air was crisp and cold, and the thick rug he tucked around her was very welcome.

He flicked the reins and clicked his tongue to the horse.

With a swish of runners, and the sleighbells attached to the harness jingling merrily, they were off at a trot, heading for the lakeshore through a snowy wonderland of fir- and pine-clad hills.

The experience was so delightful and unexpected that, as they followed the road which ran around the southern edge of the lake, she found herself smiling.

Slanting her a glance, he asked, 'Have you ever been in one of these before?'

'No,' she answered truthfully. 'But I think a sleigh ride's a lovely idea.'

'Then you're not sorry you came?'

'No.' She couldn't be sorry.

'Actually, I have more than just a ride in mind.'

'Oh?' She was instantly on guard.

'Don't worry—' his smile was mocking '—an elopement isn't on the agenda.'

'I never thought it was,' she denied sharply. Then, realising she'd risen nicely to his bait, she forced herself to ask evenly, 'So what is?'

'A spot of shopping. It's Christmas Day tomorrow and I still haven't got Caitlin a present. I thought perhaps you could help me choose something?'

'I'd love to,' she said eagerly. 'And I could do with getting her something myself. All I've managed so far, apart from a book of fairy stories, is to knit Barnaby a new hat and scarf.'

'That sounds like a sure-fire winner,' he remarked approvingly.

Some three quarters of an hour later they stopped at Winfellows, the main hotel in the picturesque but touristy town of Hemslock, and, leaving an ex-groom to take care of the horse, went in for lunch.

Keeping the conversation light and general, Matthew set himself out to be a charming companion, while Caroline, relaxed and contented, let down her guard and thoroughly enjoyed herself.

As soon as the meal was over they headed, on foot, for the shops. The snow was crisp and compact, making walking easy. Christmas decorations were everywhere, and the department store windows sparkled with lights and tinsel and festive goods of all kinds.

After spending more than an hour in Mason's toy department, they finally settled on a selection of things they thought would appeal to any little girl.

Though Caroline knew she was living in a cloud-cuckoo-land, being together like this, conferring over what to buy Caitlin, had made it one of the happiest times she had ever known.

Choosing paper bright with Santas and reindeers, Matthew asked for the presents to be wrapped and sent along to the hotel.

Then, instead of going straight back to Winfellows, as she had expected, he said purposefully that they had something else to buy.

They took the elevator up one floor, and, suddenly realising they were in the fur department, she darted him a look of alarm.

'Why are we—?'

He cut her off in mid-sentence. 'Because I intend to buy you something warm to wear.'

'No!' Digging in her toes, she refused to move. 'I don't want you to buy me anything.'

Turning, Matthew gripped her upper arms, his fingers biting in, and with a composure so rigid she knew it was a warning, he said quietly, 'Before you start panicking, will you listen to me, Caroline? This isn't payment for services rendered—if it were I would be buying you mink—nor are there any strings attached. This is simply a small Christmas gift.'

'I hate fur,' she told him shakily.

'Then you can choose something in the fun-fur range.'

His hand gripping her elbow, he propelled her forward and selected a beautiful coat that to her untrained eye looked like mink. Opening it, he displayed the label, which read, 'Beauty Without Cruelty' and stated that the pile was one hundred per cent acrylic.

Though not real fur, it was clearly expensive.

'Try it on.'

It was light and soft and luxuriously warm, and the big collar pulled forward to form a face-framing hood.

'Ideal,' he commented. 'Unless there's anything you like better?'

'No, but I really don't—'

'Then we'll take it.' To a rather supercilious saleslady who had materialised by their side, he said crisply, 'Don't bother to wrap it. My fiancée will keep it on.'

Flurried, but grateful that he'd been thoughtful enough to give her the status of fiancée, Caroline was shepherded to the pay-desk.

A few minutes later, her jacket in one of the store's carrier bags, they were out on the snowy sidewalk, heading back to the hotel.

Having achieved his object, Matthew returned to being the easy, entertaining companion who had made her day so enjoyable, and, forgetting her discomfort over the coat, Caroline found herself once again responding to the warmth of his charm.

They had a pot of tea at Winfellows before piling their packages into the sleigh and setting off back along the quiet lakeside road.

The sun had gone, and the sky had turned to an icy pearl laced with grey ribbons of cloud. As dusk crept stealthily out of hiding their lamps gleamed yellow on the banks of snow bordering the road.

Enfolded in the soft warmth of Matthew's gift, Caroline watched the Christmas-card scenery and listened to the muffled clip-clop of the horse's hooves, secure in a rainbow bubble of happiness.

'How old was your husband when he died?'

Matthew's sudden query shattered her happiness as a hammerblow shattered glass.

'Wh—what?'

He repeated the question.

Wits scattered, she spoke the truth. 'He was twenty-four.'

'Tragically young,' Matthew commented. 'Tony, my stepbrother, was only that age.' Then he asked softly, 'What did your husband die of?'

After a moment's hesitation, her voice hoarse, she answered, 'He had a very rare form of cancer.'

Just for an instant Matthew looked startled, then, his face wiped clear of expression, he said, 'Tony was killed in a car crash. His wife was driving. God knows why he allowed her to, because it was snowing, the roads were bad, and she was in no fit state to be behind a wheel.'

With quiet desperation, Caroline said, 'You sound as if you think the accident was her fault.'

'I don't blame her for the *accident*...that couldn't be helped. They skidded on black ice and hit the concrete pier of a road bridge. But Tony was thrown through the

windscreen. It came out later at the inquest that when
she insisted on driving they changed seats, and he failed
to fasten his safety belt.

'So I certainly think she was to blame for his death...'

She was to blame for his death... The accusation
seemed to ricochet inside Caroline's head, and she
pressed her gloved fingers against her temples.

The shock of Matthew's damning indictment was all
the greater because of her previous happiness, and she
sat perfectly still, every breath a stab of agony, as though
she'd been shut in an iron maiden, unable to do or say
anything to alleviate the pain.

Tony had always been careless over fastening his seat
belt, and usually she'd reminded him, but that night she
couldn't have done so.

So Matthew was right. In a way she *was* to blame for
Tony's death.

She gave a little moan of despair.

'Are you all right?' Matthew demanded sharply.

Through stiff lips, she answered, 'Yes, I'm quite all
right.'

'I thought that my reminding you of your husband
might have bothered you?'

'I've just got a bit of a headache.'

'It's not too severe, I hope?' Though solicitous, his
words held a warning. 'It was my intention to take you
to the Christmas Eve party tonight.'

Five minutes ago, even though she had nothing suitable to wear, she would have found the prospect of going
to the party with him a wonderfully exciting one.

Now, her lovely day in ruins, she dreaded the thought
of having to try and act as if nothing was wrong.

But, recalling his earlier words—'If I ask for your
company...I expect to get it'—she bit her lip, before
saying jerkily, 'When we get back I'll take a headache pill.'

Matthew made no comment, and apart from the creak of the harness and the sounds made by the sleigh they travelled the next few miles in silence, while Caroline sat still and blank-eyed, submerged in thought.

It had never occurred to her that Matthew would blame her for Tony's death, and the shock had been catastrophic.

With no chance of defending herself, of explaining why she'd done what she had, it was yet another crime to add to her sins, she thought bleakly.

Perhaps she should never have taken this job. If she hadn't it would have saved a great deal of hurt and misery. But then she would never have known her daughter, never spent those moments of delight in Matthew's arms.

No, no matter what it cost, she couldn't regret it. Even though the memory of that night, the look of despair on Tony's young, handsome face, had now returned to haunt her...

During the first six months of their marriage, looking forward eagerly to the birth of 'his' child, Tony lost his air of brooding melancholy. In spite of the shabby apartment, their lack of money and his concern over Kate having to work, he was more cheerful than she'd ever known him.

Grace, delighted by the news that she was to be a grandmother, remarked on how different Tony seemed, saying, 'You can tell that having a wife suits him. I've never seen him look so happy.'

John and Julie Jefferson, young married friends of theirs, who lived in Morningside Heights, also commented that being an expectant father agreed with him.

'He used to be a miserable devil to work with,' John said humorously. 'Now he's positively exuberant.'

But then, finally, Kate was forced to give up her job.

Their financial problems increased alarmingly and Tony started to look pale and drawn again, and perpetually worried.

Concerned for them both, unable to understand why Tony obstinately refused to ask his stepbrother for help, his mother did as much as she could, but he continued to look tired and ill.

Visiting them one Sunday, Grace remarked to her son, 'You really don't look at all well. I do wish you'd see a doctor.'

'I've been trying to persuade him to,' Kate agreed. 'Perhaps he'll do it to please you.'

'There's nothing wrong with me,' Tony said irritably. 'I just get weary, and my bones ache. Going to and from work on the subway is enough to wear anyone out.'

'I've just had a marvellous idea,' Grace cried excitedly. 'These days when I go anywhere I nearly always take a taxi. I very seldom use my car. So what if I give it to you as a Christmas present? You'll need transport when the baby arrives...'

'It would be great to have our own car.' Tony sounded wistful. 'But I doubt if we could afford to run it.'

'I'll help to pay the running costs for the time being,' Grace told him. 'On condition that you go and see a doctor.'

Tony used the car to take him to the Groober Hospital on the Lower West Side, after his doctor had referred him to a specialist there.

He'd refused to mention the hospital appointment to his mother, saying it would only upset her, and when Grace had asked him point-blank what the doctor had said, he'd answered, 'He told me I was a bit anaemic. Nothing to worry about.'

The following Friday, the day the results of his various tests would be through, the Jeffersons were giving a Christmas party, and Kate and Tony had been invited.

Knowing the baby was almost due, Kate had cried off—though she had encouraged Tony to accept, hoping it might cheer him up and give him something different to think about.

On Friday afternoon he left the office early in order to keep his four o'clock appointment with the specialist. 'I'll go with you,' Kate offered, seeing he was nervous.

He shook his head. 'These big boys are seldom on time. It will only mean you hanging around for ages. You stay here and keep your feet up, like the gynaecologist said.'

The instant the door had closed behind him, Kate wished she'd insisted.

He was gone for what seemed an eternity, and with growing concern, anxious and unable to settle, she waited and listened for his key in the lock.

It was well after seven before she heard it, and the moment he walked into the apartment Kate knew her anxiety had been justified.

His face was ghastly, his eyes like two dark holes poked in a white sheet.

'What's wrong?' she whispered.

Sinking down on the settee by her side, he told her. 'They say it's a very rare and pernicious form of cancer, and, though I may get a period of remission, my chances of living until the baby's three months old are slim.'

'No... No! With all the advances in medical science there must be *something* they can do...'

'No doubt they'll try, but the specialist refused to hold out what he called "false hopes."'

Putting her arms around him, Kate cradled his head to her breast. 'Well, I won't give up hope,' she said fiercely. 'I want you to live to see our baby grow up.'

For a while they sat in silence, then he said, 'Even if I don't, I want you to know that marrying you was the best thing I ever did. These last few months have been the happiest of my adult life.'

Then, with a kind of spurious gaiety, he went on, 'Well, if I haven't got long, I've some living to do. You don't mind if I leave you for an hour or two?'

He'd already been drinking, she could smell the bourbon on his breath, and, her mouth dry, she asked, 'Where are you going?'

'John and Julie's party—remember?'

'You'll take a cab, won't you?'

'We haven't money to waste on a cab.' His expression was mulish, and she realised he'd had more to drink than she'd suspected. 'I'm not in my coffin yet. I'm perfectly capable of driving.'

Well aware that if she tried to persuade him he would only get more stubborn, she said as casually as possible, 'You know, I'm fed up with the apartment. I think I'll come with you.'

For a moment he looked surprised, then he said with a terrible twisted smile, 'That's my girl. Make the most of my company while I'm still here.'

She had hoped that by going with him she could get him to change his mind about taking a cab, but when they got outside he helped her into their car, ignoring her pleas, and climbed behind the wheel.

It was snowing as they set off for Morningside Heights. They didn't talk. All at once there seemed to be nothing left to say.

When they reached the Jeffersons' tiny apartment, the party was hotting up. Julie, small and dark and vivacious, opened the door and, though obviously surprised to see Kate, cried, 'Come on in, you guys, and join the festivities!'

She took their coats, and after a quick, searching glance at both their faces, led Kate into the kitchen while Tony headed for the bar.

Pushing her into a comfortable rocking chair, Julie demanded, 'Have you two had a row?'

'No.'

'Then what's wrong? Why did Tony walk away as though he couldn't wait to get a drink in his hand?'

Filled with a kind of numb anguish, Kate told her.

'Oh, my God,' Julie whispered.

'I don't know how we'll break the news to his mother,' Kate said. 'Grace adores him. She'll be devastated.'

Suddenly the tears came.

When she was all cried out, Julie said, 'Look, you'd better come and lie down on my bed. I'll have to go and circulate, but I'll get John to keep an eye on Tony.'

Isolated in misery, Kate lay staring blindly into the darkness, listening to the voices and music and laughter coming from the next room, until eventually the noise began to lessen and Julie returned to say the party was breaking up.

'We have something of a problem. John wanted to call a cab, but Tony is insisting on driving himself. He's waiting in the car now, but he's very drunk, so you'll have to stop him.'

When Kate had hurriedly pulled on her coat, John accompanied her outside. 'It's slippy underfoot, so you'd better hold on to my arm.'

Reaching the car, they found the engine running and Tony half slumped over the wheel. 'Come on, old son,' John urged. 'You're in no fit state to drive. Get out, and I'll call you and Kate a cab.'

Lifting his head, Tony muttered thickly, belligerently, 'I'm not getting out. We're taking the car.'

'Then move over and let me drive,' Kate begged.

When, to her surprise and relief, he did, she got in hastily. The only thought in her mind to get him safely home, she set off down Tahlequah Street towards the overpass...

'If you don't mind walking from the stables?' Matthew's voice broke into her dark thoughts.

'No, I don't mind.' Jerked back to the present, Caroline answered the half-heard question.

They were just entering the spa complex. To the right she could see the lights of the main buildings and the towering Christmas tree.

Reaching the lantern-lit stables, they gathered up the various parcels and, having thanked the man in charge, set off to walk the comparatively short distance to the chalet.

When Matthew opened the door into the living-room, Caroline saw that a six-foot Christmas tree and a large box of decorations had been delivered in their absence.

'I thought that when Caitlin's back we could decorate the tree and put the presents under it,' he suggested.

'Yes, she'll enjoy helping.' Caroline had been looking forward to joining in the pleasure that Christmas brought, but now her cheerfulness was forced.

'First, however, I must go over to Reception. Later tonight I've a visitor dropping in briefly, so I'll need to know what time he's likely to be here.'

There was something, some nuance in Matthew's voice, that made her glance at him sharply.

His smile holding a soft, menacing quality, he added, 'It's someone I thought you might like to meet.'

All at once, without knowing why, Caroline felt alarmed, apprehensive, and, watching him walk to the door, she shivered.

CHAPTER SEVEN

WHEN Matthew had gone, her head pounding, Caroline swallowed a couple of painkillers and went to take a hot bath, hoping it would relax her.

She had just finished dressing in a fine wool skirt and jumper when she heard Matthew's voice, then a moment later Caitlin calling excitedly, 'Caro, Caro, come quick.'

As soon as she went through to the living-room, Caitlin came trotting up and thrust a large, flat box gift-wrapped in red and gold, into her hands. 'Barnaby and me buyed you this...and we did write a card,' she added importantly.

'Oh, thank you, darling.' Down on her haunches, Caroline hugged the small figure. 'How lovely of you both.'

Jumping up and down with glee, Caitlin urged, 'Open it. Open it.'

'If it's a Christmas present it should go under the tree until tomorrow.'

'Daddy said open it *now*.'

A nod from Matthew confirmed that, so Caroline opened the envelope tucked beneath the bow. There were several large, wobbly scrawls across the card, and written in Matthew's decisive hand, 'With love from Caitlin and Barnaby H. Bear.'

'Barnaby *H*. Bear?' she asked him with amusement.

'You should know that all American bears have a middle name.'

'So what does the H stand for?' she queried.

Straight-faced, he told her, 'Hairy.'

113

She gave a little gurgle of laughter, then with Caitlin's help removed the ribbon and the wrapping from the box.

Inside, nestling in folds of tissue paper, was a drift of aquamarine silk chiffon. With trembling hands Caroline lifted out an exquisitely cut ankle-length evening dress, the exact colour of her eyes.

'Do you like it?' Caitlin demanded.

'It's beautiful,' Caroline said unsteadily.

'We buyed more, didn't we, Daddy?' Caitlin hopped from foot to foot excitedly.

Matthew produced a smallish oblong box, similarly wrapped, and, as though he knew the meagreness of Caroline's wardrobe, said lightly, 'We thought you might need some accessories.'

It contained a pair of silver sandals and a small matching bag.

'Barnaby and me did choose them,' Caitlin informed her proudly.

'Thank you, darling.' Caroline kissed the small face turned up to her.

'Kiss Barnaby…'

When Barnaby had been soundly kissed on his big black nose, Caitlin added, 'And Daddy.'

'Daddy's too big to be kissed,' Caroline objected hurriedly.

'He's not too big…are you, Daddy?'

'Certainly not.' With a gleam in his eyes that acknowledged Caroline's discomfort, Matthew waited.

Having no option, she stood on tiptoe and touched her lips to his cheek in a brief caress.

He gave her a mocking smile before asking, 'Now, where shall we put the Christmas tree? In the corner or by the window?'

'By the window, I think.'

Caroline's headache had lifted, and, trying determinedly to push everything but the enjoyment of this

moment from her mind, she helped Caitlin to unpack the
box of decorations while Matthew manhandled the
heavy tree into position.

Amidst much excitement, it was adorned with strings
of lights and baubles and shining tinsel. When every
branch glittered, Matthew lifted Caitlin so she could
place the star, somewhat lopsidedly, on top.

That done, he switched on the lights, and they stood
back to admire the magical sight before piling the various packages around the base of the tree.

After a glance at his watch, Matthew said to Caitlin,
'Time to get ready for bed now, poppet. I'm taking
Caroline to dinner and then to the party, so she can wear
her new dress. Gladys will be coming over to stay with
you until we get back.'

'Can I sleep with Jane, Daddy?'

'You mean over at the nursery?'

'Yes.'

'I don't see why not—if you'd rather?'

Caitlin nodded decidedly.

Filled with a sudden unease, Caroline asked hurriedly,
'But will Santa know where to find her?'

'Of course he will.' Matthew brushed the doubt aside.
'To make tonight's babysitting easier for the staff, and
also because the youngsters prefer it, there are at least
half a dozen children staying in the nursery. They'll all
be hanging up their stockings...'

'Oh, but—'

'It makes more sense, actually, and it will save Gladys
sitting here on her own all evening.'

Then he turned to Caitlin, 'In the morning, as soon as
we've had breakfast, we'll come over and collect you.
Then we can open the presents that are under the tree.
Okay?'

He was answered by another emphatic nod.

Turning back to Caroline, he asked, 'Perhaps you'll

collect Caitlin's night things, and whatever else she may need...?'

Though framed as a request, it was undoubtedly an order.

'And I'll take her over while you start to get ready.'

Seeing no help for it, Caroline did as she'd been instructed, and, having dressed Caitlin warmly, kissed her and Barnaby goodnight and waved them off.

Some half an hour later, when she emerged from her room, it was to find Matthew, already showered and dressed in impeccable evening clothes, waiting for her.

His eyes travelled slowly over her from head to toe, and a flame ignited in his tawny eyes.

Clinging subtly to every slender curve, the dress looked superb. The light bluish-green echoed the colour of her eyes and made them shine like jewels.

Ignoring his instruction to leave her hair loose, she had taken it up into a gleaming chignon, which emphasised her long neck and made the most of her bone structure.

In spite of everything she wanted to be beautiful for him, and she found herself longing for a little praise, for some word of approval.

But apart from that blazing look he gave no sign that he liked what he saw. His face curiously set and tense, he held out the coat he had bought for her that afternoon.

Without a word, she slipped it on, and allowed herself to be escorted to the door.

The major walkways were always kept clear, but new snow was falling, fine and powdery, and she was forced to step carefully in the high-heeled sandals.

They had been walking a little apart, but when Matthew offered her his arm she was only too pleased to take it.

In the spa complex the main restaurant seemed to be full of well-dressed men and bejewelled women, but the maître d' met them at the door and murmured that of course there was a table reserved for them.

Their coats were whisked away, and they were shown to a secluded alcove where they ordered immediately.

Though the place breathed simplicity, Caroline recognised that it was the kind of elegant simplicity that only a great deal of money could buy.

When the waiter had gone, Matthew, who seemed to have shrugged off whatever had been bothering him, reached across and took her hand. 'I haven't yet told you how enchanting you look.'

A warm glow brought a tinge of apricot colour to her high cheekbones. 'Thank you.' His touch making her heart beat faster, she added a shade breathlessly, 'It's all due to the dress.'

'Now, there I must disagree.' His voice was husky, and he held her hand for a moment longer before releasing it.

He might not *like* her, but there was no doubt that a strong, if unwilling physical attraction still existed.

While they ate lake trout with almonds, and drank a well-chilled white wine from the Napa Valley, Matthew became the charming, intellectual companion he'd been over lunch. Looking relaxed and benign, he kept her entertained with vivid word-pictures of the Orient, which he knew well.

Though still off balance after a day which, with its highs and lows, had been rather like riding on a see-saw, Caroline made a determined effort to put Tony's drawn face out of her mind, and soon her spirits began to lift a little.

By the time the meal was over, she felt almost light-hearted, and for the first time found herself looking forward to the evening ahead.

Talking easily, they lingered over their coffee and brandy, until, with a glance at his watch, Matthew remarked, 'I guess we'd better join the party. As I mentioned earlier, there's someone dropping in that I'd like you to meet.'

Hearing again that faint undercurrent of tension, she looked at him uneasily, but his expression was bland and unrevealing.

They reached the ballroom, which was lavishly decorated and hung with huge swags of spruce and holly, to find the party was in full swing.

There was a well-stocked bar, and tables were scattered around the edge of the polished floor. On a raised dais at the far end of the room a small orchestra was playing a Gershwin medley. The lights had been dimmed, and a fair number of people were dancing.

Matthew turned to Caroline, and without a word being spoken she went into his arms.

She had never danced with him before, but their steps fitted and, as though made for each other, their two bodies melded into one harmonious whole.

Wishing it could last for ever, Caroline gave herself up to the bliss of the moment, and, with his cheek resting against her hair, they danced as if they were the only two people on the floor.

When the music stopped it was like wakening from a lovely dream. She blinked and smiled at him. Just for an instant he looked at her as he had done the first night they'd met.

An arm around her waist, he was escorting her to a table that had been reserved for them when a man's voice said, 'So there you are! I was beginning to think I'd have to go without seeing you.'

Caroline turned to look at the speaker, and found herself staring at a ghost.

He was about her height, with a thin, sensitive face, black curly hair and hazel eyes.

Shock hit her like an express train. There was a roar-

ing noise in her ears and darkness enveloped her. Only
Matthew's arm tightening around her stopped her slipping to the floor.

When Caroline opened her eyes, she was lying on a
couch in a living-room that was oddly familiar. As her
head began to clear she realised they were in Matthew's
private apartment in the main complex.

He was sitting by her side, his eyes fixed on her face,
his expression taut. 'How do you feel?' He sounded
shaken, his voice harsh with a strange mixture of anger
and anxiety.

'I'm all right,' she managed to answer.

'You gave me quite a shock,' he muttered.

She shivered. It could have been nothing compared to
the shock she'd experienced. But she couldn't admit
that.

'I'm sorry...' Needing to explain her faint, she said
with an attempt at lightness, 'It was quite hot in there,
and I should never have had that brandy. I have no head
for spirits...'

Taking a deep breath, she added, 'I'm sorry if I made
a fool of myself in front of...everybody.'

'I doubt if many people noticed—apart from Derek.'

*Derek Newman... Tony's cousin and best man... The
family likeness was so strong that just for an instant
she'd thought she was looking at a ghost.*

Hands clenched, she made herself wait a few seconds
before she asked, 'He was the man you wanted me to
meet?'

Matthew's face tightened, but he said merely, 'Yes.'

A shiver ran through her. Had Matthew arranged the
meeting on purpose, hoping she would betray herself?

No, surely not. That would mean he knew who
she was.

Perhaps he did. Maybe he was playing some cat and mouse game, waiting for her nerve to crack.

No, surely he couldn't be so cruel?

Her heart thumping, she knew he *could*.

He *hated* Kate, and it was easy to be cruel to someone you hated.

But he was going on, 'Derek is Caitlin's second cousin, and apart from her mother I believe he's her nearest living relative.

'I haven't seen him for quite some time. He's been working in Nova Scotia, but now he's heading south. His long-time girlfriend lives in Calow, and he's on his way there to spend Christmas with her. When he knew I'd be at Clear Lake, he said he'd drop in just briefly on his way past.'

Caroline sat up and, bracing herself, asked, 'Is he still here?'

'No, he had to get on. The weather's closing in and he didn't want to get stranded.'

Trying to hide her relief that he'd gone, she said, 'I'm sorry I messed up his visit.'

Matthew shook his head. 'It served its purpose...'

Her blood ran cold.

'He wanted to leave a Christmas present for Caitlin—' A knock cut through his words. 'Ah, this will be the tea I sent for.' Rising to his feet, he went to the door.

'Thanks. Yes, she's fine now,' Caroline heard him say. 'No I'm sure there's no need for a doctor. It was just the heat in the ballroom.'

Returning with a tray of tea, he put it on a low table and poured a cup, adding a generous amount of sugar.

'I don't take sugar,' she objected.

Stirring it in, he said firmly, 'Sweet tea is good for any kind of shock or faintness.'

About to protest further, she had second thoughts and began to sip the hot liquid he'd handed to her.

It was very welcome, and more palatable than she'd expected. By the time the cup was empty, she was feeling considerably steadier.

Returning it to the tray, Matthew sat down again beside her, his hip touching hers, and picked up her hand, his fingertips pressing lightly against her inner wrist.

'That's better,' he murmured with satisfaction. 'Your pulse is back to normal and you've got a little colour in your cheeks.'

His scrutiny made her colour deepen.

Suddenly scared of his closeness, and the effect it was having on her, she pulled her wrist free and remarked jerkily, 'It's still quite early. If you'd like to go back to the party...?'

'I'm no longer in a party mood. What about you?'

'I—I thought I'd go to bed.'

'That sounds like an excellent idea.' His voice was deep and husky.

Her breathing becoming shallow, impeded, she said, 'I just need my coat...' Then she realised that her feet were bare. 'And my sandals.'

He shook his head. 'I've decided we'll stay here. I don't want you to have to turn out again on a night like this.'

With soft, purposeful movements, he began to take the pins from her chignon. As the silky hair tumbled around her shoulders he leaned forward to kiss her. His eyes were closed, the thick, dark lashes brushing his hard cheeks.

The sight brought an insidious rush of tenderness. Trying to fight it, she closed her own eyes.

But as he kissed her gently, sweetly, as if it was the most natural thing in the world, lack of sight only served to intensify the feeling his lips moving against hers was creating.

Gritting her teeth, she did her best to fight the singing

sweetness that was melting her resolve and filling her
heart with love and longing.

She knew the feeling was all on her side, that he didn't
love her, yet when he was kissing her as though she was
all he wanted in the world, she felt an overwhelming
urge to believe he did.

But that was the worst kind of self-deception.

Turning her head sharply, she cried, '*Please*,
Matthew!'

Her sudden impassioned plea seemed to shock him,
and, his hands lightly gripping her upper arms, he drew
back to look at her.

Trembling, she made a pathetic attempt to free herself.

He wouldn't allow it. Drawing her gently into his
arms, he ran his hands up and down her back in a curiously soothing gesture.

'You want me as much as I want you. Why try to
fight it? What are you afraid of?'

*Of not being loved. Of being hurt. Humiliated. Des-
pised. So many things.*

'What am I to you?' she asked shakily.

'Every man has a weakness.' His dark face hardened.
'Let's say you're mine.'

'Not merely a woman who's available when you want
one?'

For an instant he looked angry, then he said almost
wearily, 'If only it was as simple as that, then neither of
us would need to worry. There's no lack of available
women. Unfortunately it seems no other woman will do.'

His mouth, a beautiful mouth, severe yet sensual,
moved closer.

Involuntarily she stiffened.

Faintly mocking, he said, 'I'm only going to kiss you,
nothing terrible. Afterwards, if you still want to say
no...' He left the sentence unfinished.

This time when he covered her mouth with his own

her lips were a little parted. Kissing her persuasively, ardently, he coaxed them further apart and deepened the kiss.

Liquid fire ran through her veins like molten lava, burning her up, destroying her few shaky defences.

When at last he lifted his head her eyes were still closed. 'Caroline?' He spoke her name softly, and, sitting quite still, put his palm against her cheek.

Opening heavy lids, she gazed up at him. His expression was tense and waiting. He really was, she realised dazedly, leaving the decision to her.

If she gave in now she would be lost for ever, his to command. But wasn't she his anyway? He held her heart and she would never be free to love another man.

With a little murmur of acceptance, she signalled her surrender by turning her lips into the warmth of his palm.

His face blazing with passion and triumph, he picked her up in his arms and carried her through to the bedroom she remembered from nearly four long years ago.

With urgent hands he undressed her and laid her down on the big bed, before stripping off his own clothes.

When he bent to kiss her, she put her arms around his neck, the blood drumming in her ears, and drew him down to her, longing for the touch of his hands.

Nothing mattered any longer—not his occasional unkindness and deliberate cruelty, not even the fear of being hurt and rejected, of losing her self-respect. Filled with a kind of wild happiness, all she could feel was a deep and abiding thankfulness that he was here with her.

As though they couldn't get enough of each other, in a spinning world without beginning or end they made love, their entire beings burning in a fever that took most of the night to spend.

The following morning Caroline awoke to instant and

complete remembrance, and for a while lay with her eyes
closed, hugging her happiness to her.

The night spent in his arms had been complete and
fulfilling, a loving union that had touched many levels,
that had been as much spiritual as physical.

With a little sigh, she reached out to him, but she was
alone in the big bed.

Throwing back the duvet, she pulled on a silk robe
that was lying over a chair and went to the window to
draw back the curtains and look out at the glistening
white world.

During the hours of darkness the snow had stopped
falling and Christmas morning had dawned bright and
clear. The most wonderful Christmas morning she had
ever known, gift-wrapped in gladness and joy.

Her heart so light she could have burst into song, she
went through to the bathroom, where a search through
the cabinet provided a cellophane-wrapped toothbrush
and a tube of toothpaste.

When she had cleaned her teeth and showered, she
ran a borrowed comb through her hair and donned the
robe once more, deciding it was more suited to the
breakfast table than an evening dress.

Wearing dark trousers and a roll-necked sweater,
Matthew was in the kitchenette pouring coffee. Though
Caroline's feet were bare, and made no discernible
sound, he turned at her approach.

'Good morning.' She smiled at him and, her face
glowing with love and happiness, prepared to walk into
his arms.

'Good morning.' His expression was guarded and his
voice coolly polite. There was none of the warmth she
had expected. 'I was about to bring you some coffee.'

Hiding her bewilderment as best she could, she accepted a cup, managing to match his tone with an
equally polite, 'Thank you.'

As they sipped he informed her, 'To speed things up, I've ordered breakfast…'

She had visualised making breakfast herself, and then their eating in leisurely and loving intimacy before they went together to fetch Caitlin.

A second or two later there was a knock, and, raising his voice, Matthew called, 'Come in!'

A young man wheeled in a loaded trolley, and with deftness and efficiency transferred its contents to the table.

When he'd gone Matthew pulled out a chair for Caroline with a kind of studied civility, before taking his own seat.

Uncovering the various dishes, he queried, 'What would you like?' He could have been addressing a total stranger.

Wanting to hide the fact that her appetite had vanished, she plumped for a couple of slices of the thin crispy bacon and a hash brown, and made a pretence of eating.

Matthew chose scrambled eggs and, his dark face aloof, proceeded to eat in silence. There was a tautness in his manner, a brooding purpose—hidden, as yet, but as potentially dangerous as an unexploded bomb.

After a while, unable to bear the tension any longer, she remarked with false brightness, 'It's turned out to be a lovely morning.'

He made no reply, and his brief underbrow glance seemed to dismiss both her and her attempt at conversation as unimportant.

Cut to the heart by that look of indifference, she blurted out, 'I don't understand why you're so distant, so angry…'

Lifting his head, he looked fully at her.

'Last night I thought…' Her courage shrivelling, the

whispered words tailed off. Desperately, she asked, 'What's *wrong*?'

His eyes cool and very green, he answered, 'Nothing's *wrong*, exactly. It's just that the cold light of day puts a different complexion on things.' With a wry twist to his lips, he continued, 'Returning sanity strongly suggests that last night should never have happened.'

So he was having second thoughts, as he had done that night in his house. Once again she could hear him asking, 'Regretting it?' And her own response, 'Should I be?'

Then, like a deathblow, had come his answer. 'Perhaps we both should.'

All hope dying, she sat, stricken, while her spirits descended in a sickening spiral of despair.

How foolish of her to imagine that last night might have changed anything. That feeling of complete and loving fulfilment hadn't been mutual; it had been all on her side. Oh, yes, he'd wanted her, but for him the satisfaction had been merely physical. And short-lived.

Studying her, he observed dispassionately, 'From the moment I first kissed you I knew there'd be trouble...and I was right. Look what it's led to.'

Trying to hide how much she'd been hurt, she said stiltedly, 'You sound as if you blame me.'

'I do.'

'I didn't *ask* you to kiss me,' she protested hoarsely. 'And if we hadn't been caught in that blizzard...'

'Ah, but we were.'

'That wasn't my fault. I wanted to go straight down.'

Mocking her, he said, 'You sound as if you blame me.'

'I do.'

'For misjudging the weather?'

'It was something that shouldn't have happened.'

His white teeth gleamed in a smile. 'You think I got us trapped purposely? Engineered the whole thing?'

She was about to say no when something about the way he'd spoken, the mocking gleam in his eyes, revived her earlier suspicions.

'I think the situation was of your making.'

Instead of refuting the suggestion, he admitted coolly, 'You're quite right.'

She drew a deep, shaky breath. 'You planned the whole thing in cold blood, seduced me deliberately, just so you could lay a ghost!' Then she went on angrily, 'How *can* you begin to blame me?'

'Men have been putting the blame on women ever since Eve tempted Adam.'

'But that isn't *fair*,' she choked.

'Where is it written that life has to be fair?'

When she made no answer, he went on evenly, 'But, you see, the problem is this: the plan didn't work.' His voice had a soft, dangerous quality. 'I didn't succeed in laying Kate's ghost...rather the reverse. Which makes life...shall we say...difficult...'

Knowing there was more to come, she watched him with apprehensive eyes while with calm deliberation he refilled both their coffee cups.

'I believe I told you that I was hoping to adopt Caitlin?'

Her heart in her mouth, Caroline nodded.

'And I can't afford to jeopardise my chances.' His voice was crisp now, decided. 'Bearing that in mind, I don't think it would be politic to indulge in an affair with her nanny. What do you think?'

There was a fraught silence, then, swallowing, Caroline said jerkily, 'I agree. That's what I was trying to say yesterday.'

'So you're willing to keep our relationship as that of

employer and employee, go back to being simply a paid nanny?'

Feeling as though she was walking on shifting sands, she whispered, 'Yes.'

'I don't think it would work.'

Suddenly terribly afraid, she insisted, 'I can make it work.'

'Well, I can't,' he said flatly. 'Even if I got married—and that would make the adoption process a whole lot easier—if you were still living under my roof I doubt if I could resist the kind of temptation you offer.

'And, as I've just said, it would be neither sensible nor desirable to indulge in an ongoing affair with my daughter's nanny...' His face hardened into granite. 'That being the case, I'm afraid that when Christmas is over...' He left the sentence unfinished.

Her voice scarcely above a whisper, she said, 'You want me to leave...'

'I'll give you a month's salary in lieu of notice, and good references...'

His words were like rocks he'd hit her with; her pain was expressed in a silent cry... *No, no, he couldn't mean it...* But she knew he did.

It had seemed like a miracle when fate had offered her another chance to be with her daughter, but now, because of the ungovernable sexual attraction that still existed between Matthew and herself, she had forfeited that chance.

Even in her darkest hours Caroline had never felt such black hopelessness and desolation. She wanted to weep, to plead, but it would be useless—and far too revealing.

'Aren't you going to protest?' His eyes were bright and mocking, as though he'd read her thoughts. 'Ask me to change my mind?'

'Would it do any good?'

'You'll never know until you try.'

He was playing with her, she knew. Lifting a white, pinched face, she said bleakly, 'You'd like to hear me beg, wouldn't you?'

His smile mirthless, he admitted, 'It would give me a great deal of satisfaction.'

'And even greater satisfaction to then say no?'

'Perhaps you can guess why?'

'Because I remind you of...Kate. You can't hurt her, so I'm to serve as a whipping boy.'

'A moment or so ago you made it clear that no matter what it cost you wanted to remain working for me.'

Trying to keep her voice steady, she said, 'You've just pointed out that that wouldn't be practicable.'

'Nor would it. But you were willing to try. Why, after the way I've treated you? Any ordinary nanny would have given up and left before this.'

'I—I've grown fond of Caitlin.'

'In so short a time?'

'She's a very lovable child.'

'Surely in the general run of things a nanny can't afford to get too attached to her charges?'

'Sometimes it's difficult not to.' Her voice shook, betraying her awareness of how thin was the ice she skated on. If he was already suspicious...

'I thought your reluctance to leave might have been due to some other cause.'

'Some other cause?' she repeated.

'An interest apart from Caitlin?'

When she just stared at him, he smiled mockingly. 'From the first, your reaction to me has hardly been the normal reaction of a nanny to an employer...'

All at once she realised he was offering her a lifeline. If she admitted that her interest was in *him*...

'You must know you're the kind of man women go for,' she said jerkily.

He raised a sardonic brow. 'Are you saying you're *fond* of me?'

Refusing to be baited, she shook her head. 'It's just sexual attraction.'

'Whatever it is, it's pretty explosive. And mutual. So where does that leave us?' Before she could speak he answered his own question. 'It leaves me without a nanny and you without a job…unless…'

'Unless?' Not sure what she was hoping for, not even sure she could hope at all, and well aware that he might only be prolonging the agony, she still couldn't keep the hope out of her voice.

'Unless we solved our problems by getting married.'

Feeling as if she'd been struck by a brickbat, she gaped at him. Though he'd talked about getting married, that he should suggest marrying *her* was the last thing she had expected.

'You must see that it would be the ideal solution,' he pursued. 'It would make adoption easier, and give Caitlin the stability I've been wanting to give her.

'I'd gain a wife and a trustworthy nanny. You'd gain a home and a child you're already fond of.' He gave her an odd, glittering look. 'And a husband who could make you happy…at least in bed…'

'Then you're not talking about a marriage of convenience?'

'I'm talking about a real marriage.'

'Oh…'

'So what's your answer?'

When she continued to gaze at him in silence, he demanded a shade impatiently, 'Well?'

It would be wonderful to be his wife, a precious gift she'd never dared hope for. But at what cost? Suppose he only wanted to marry her to hurt her?

While Matthew watched her narrowly, seeing the indecision in her face, the struggle that was going on,

Caroline's emotions swung like a pendulum between longing and fear.

One second all that mattered was that she would no longer be just a nanny, who could be dismissed at any time, but Caitlin's mother and Matthew's wife, the next she was filled with misgivings, the knowledge that marrying Matthew would be as potentially dangerous as living in the middle of a minefield...

But what were the alternatives?

She could admit who she was and try to claim her daughter back...

But she had nowhere to live and no way of supporting a child. It would be madness to deprive Caitlin of a good home and a father who loved her and would take every care of her.

It was equally unthinkable to leave and never see her daughter, or the man she loved, again.

No, she had to take the chance he'd offered her...

When she raised clear aquamarine eyes full of unconscious decision Matthew knew he'd won, and his expression held a touch of triumph as he asked, 'Yes?'

Though she had no illusions that the price would be high, she agreed quietly, 'Yes, I'll marry you.'

'Good.' He nodded his satisfaction. 'Now I'd better walk over to the chalet and bring you back something to wear. Then we'll go and collect Caitlin and tell her the good news.'

CHAPTER EIGHT

THE curtains had been drawn, shutting out the snowy night, the lights were low, and the burning logs cast flickering shadows, making the atmosphere cosy and intimate.

Caroline sat on the couch next to Matthew while the distant sound of Christmas carols being sung around the huge tree outdoors filtered into the room.

After a day of fun and excitement, Caitlin was tucked up in bed and fast asleep.

As Matthew had predicted, out of all her toys and gifts the one that seemed to have pleased her most was Barnaby's new red and green striped scarf and bobble-hat, and he'd worn them throughout the day.

She had accepted Matthew's announcement that Caroline was to be her new mummy with matter-of-fact pleasure, on the surface more excited by the presents that Santa Claus had left her.

Instead of them all going back to the chalet, as Caroline had expected, Matthew had given instructions that their belongings, including the Christmas tree, should be moved to his suite in the main building.

'As we're going to be married, my original concern, that there are only two bedrooms here, is no longer a consideration...' Green eyes glinting, he'd added, 'Unless, of course, you would prefer not to share my bed before we're man and wife?'

Though a little flustered at the way he was forcing her hand, having already irrevocably committed herself, and unable to forego the joyful prospect of spending the nights in his arms, she shook her head.

A strange expression flitted across his face and was instantly gone. But in the space of a heartbeat she had seen that his need was as deep as her own.

His voice, however, was practical, dispassionate, as he said, 'Then I'd like you, for the sake of propriety, to be wearing my ring. I suggest we go and choose one straight away...'

She was startled both by the swift rush of pleasure the thought gave her, and the speed at which Matthew was sweeping her along.

'Klein Kimberley are the best jewellers in the complex, so if you would like to look at what they have...?'

'Surely they'll be closed?' She sounded as dazed as she felt.

'This is a private transaction that should take only a short time.'

'But it's Christmas Day.'

'The owner happens to be an old friend of mine. I'll give him a call and ask Gladys to stay with Caitlin for half an hour.'

With a kind of tolerant cynicism, he added, 'If Gladys knows of our engagement it will be a good way of spreading the news amongst the staff.'

By the time they reached the shop, a tall, nice-looking man of about forty, with fair wavy hair, was waiting for them.

Grinning broadly, he slapped Matthew on the back. 'Congratulations! You kept this a secret.'

'It was a fairly sudden decision,' Matthew admitted. Then he turned to Caroline. 'Darling, I'd like you to meet Robert Klein.'

Smiling, she said, 'How do you do?' When they'd shaken hands, she added, 'I feel terribly guilty, disturbing you on what should be a holiday.'

'Think nothing of it. I can quite understand why Matt can't wait to get a ring on your finger.'

Turning to the younger man, he asked, 'What do you have in mind? We have one or two exceptional stones.'

'I thought an aquamarine.'

'Yes.' Klein nodded. 'I can see why.'

Caroline's fingers were very slender and there were only two rings her size. The first had a single brilliant stone, the second was larger and flanked by diamonds.

'Which do you prefer?' Matthew asked.

'The solitaire,' she answered huskily.

'A good choice,' Klein agreed. 'The colour's better and it's a finer gem.'

Taking the ring from its tray, Matthew slid it onto her finger, and then, making her heart swell with happiness, lifted her hand to his lips.

'Now it's official, I think an engagement gift would be in order.'

'You've already given me more than enough,' she objected. 'And I haven't even bought you a Christmas present.'

Ignoring her protest, he leaned towards Klein and murmured something in his ear.

'Yes, I have,' the jeweller said.

He disappeared into the back of the shop and returned a few moments later with a flat, oblong leather case, which Matthew slipped into his pocket.

'Thanks. I'll write you a cheque for them both.'

'Tomorrow will do,' Klein said easily, and the two men shook hands.

Matthew put his arm around Caroline's waist, and like someone in a dream she found herself being escorted back to their suite.

When they had thanked Gladys and shown her the ring, she departed, flushed with excitement and obviously thrilled to have played some small part in the proceedings.

She had been gone only a few minutes when there

was a knock at the door and a beribboned bottle of champagne was delivered, with the compliments of the staff.

Having thanked the emissary, Matthew turned to Caroline with a wry grin. 'There, what did I tell you?'

He found two champagne flutes, and, easing off the cork with a pop, poured the sparkling wine. When he'd put a glass in her hand, he said, 'Here's to us...to *really* getting to know one another.'

Perhaps his rider should have made her wary, but, after being in the depths of despair, all she could feel was an almost incredulous joy.

It hardly seemed possible that she and Matthew were engaged and going to be married. And the fact that they were standing sipping champagne together made the situation no more believable—rather, it heightened Caroline's feeling of unreality and made her want to pinch herself...

Even now, some eight hours later, sitting on the settee next to Matthew, listening to the Christmas carols being sung, that sense of unreality persisted.

As though reading her mind, he turned to her, remarking, 'It's been quite a day, and I still haven't given you this...'

Reaching for his jacket, he felt in the pocket and took out the flat, oblong box Robert Klein had handed him. His eyes on her face, his voice dropping to almost a purr, he queried, 'Weren't you curious to know what I chose especially for you?'

Something in his tone caused her to feel a faint foreboding. But with all the excitement and pleasure of watching Caitlin open her Christmas presents, Caroline hadn't given Matthew's engagement gift a thought.

When she admitted as much, he observed, 'Almost any other woman would have reminded me, or asked what it was...'

Flicking open the lid with his thumbnail, he lifted out a necklet of red-gold, each link made by a pair of exquisitely formed clasped hands.

'It's beautiful,' she commented, 'and very unusual.'

'Try it on. It needs to fit.'

After examining it, she admitted, 'I can't see how it unfastens.'

'Let me.' A moment later it was sitting comfortably at the base of her slender throat.

'Perfect,' he approved softly.

All at once his expression—triumphant, a little cruel—alarmed and disturbed her.

Getting up, she went to the mirror.

On her, the necklet had changed from being simply a piece of jewellery into something that looked primitive, oddly barbaric, as though she was wearing some kind of fetter.

She gave an involuntary shiver. 'I've never seen anything quite like it.'

'It's a copy of an Inca betrothal necklet. Peruvian legend has it that a Quechua—a lord, or royal person—had it made specially for his bride as a symbol of ownership, rather than a ring...'

The breath caught in her throat, she asked, 'Why not a ring?'

'Because a ring she could have taken off and then replaced... You see she was a woman like Kate, and he couldn't trust her not to stray...'

While she waited, like a victim at the guillotine, Matthew paused and smiled grimly before going on. 'Once fastened, the only way she could have removed the necklet was by having it cut off.'

An icy chill ran down her spine. When she thought she could keep her voice level, Caroline queried, 'Do you mean to say this doesn't come off?'

'Oh, yes, *this* one comes off,' Matthew said. 'But then

you're not like Kate, are you?' Smoothly, he added, 'It's only necessary to know how the catch works.'

'Then please will you take it off for me?'

Reaching out, he circled her wrist and pulled her down beside him again, but when she lifted her long hair and half bent her head, he asked consideringly, 'Does it feel uncomfortable?'

'No,' she admitted. Any discomfort it caused would be purely mental.

'So why not wear it…at least until bedtime?'

She bit her lip, but, sensing he was waiting for her to protest, said nothing.

After a moment, with that swift change of topic she was never quite prepared for, he remarked, 'Now we're alone we ought to have a talk about the future…'

Lifting apprehensive eyes to his face, she waited.

'I'd like Caitlin to have brothers and sisters. I take it you have no objection? During that first interview you told me you liked children?'

Pleasure mingling with a lingering uneasiness, she agreed, 'Yes, I do.'

'However, I think we should have some time together first, to become a family and give Caitlin a chance to accept you as her mother.'

Then, as unexpected as an ambush, he went on, 'You've never asked what happened to her real mother…'

'Well, I…I…'

'You have to be the least curious woman I've ever met.' His voice could have cut glass.

When Caroline said nothing he went on, his tawny eyes on her face. 'Would it surprise you to know that she just abandoned the child?'

'No!' It was a cry of pain.

'You sound very certain.'

'I can't believe any woman would willingly abandon her own child.'

'Then why do you suppose she disappeared?'

'She must have had some pressing reason.'

Matthew's lip curled. 'You sound almost sympathetic.'

'There are always two sides to everything.'

'The only side she cared about was her own. Tony was dead, and rather than look after the child he didn't live to see, she took off and left his elderly mother, a woman with a bad heart, to take the responsibility.'

No, it wasn't like that! Caroline thought passionately. It *wasn't*.

'How can you feel any sympathy for someone like that?' Matthew had come full circle.

Sick and shaken, she stayed silent.

He gave her a cold, inimical glance. 'Finding it impossible to defend her?'

Caroline's spirit, that core of steel which had supported her through the darkest moments of her life, urged her to keep fighting. But, realising belatedly what dangerous ground she was on, she merely asked, 'Are you saying her actions are indefensible?'

'That's exactly what I'm saying—' A knock cut through his words.

Matthew got to his feet and went to the door.

'I'm terribly sorry to bother you, Mr Carran,' a man's voice said urgently, 'but there's a fire started in one of the back-up generators...'

'I'd better come and take a look.' The door clicked shut behind him.

Caroline sighed. Maybe the interruption had been for the best. If the conversation had gone on she might have betrayed herself.

She found it hard to accept that Matthew had condemned her out of hand, without showing the slightest trace of understanding or compassion.

It had been a dreadful time. Pressured, and under a great emotional strain, still too ill to think clearly, she had done what she'd thought was the best for the child, for Tony's mother—who had been devastated by her son's death—and for Matthew and the woman he'd been planning to marry.

She had never ceased to regret it, and always at the back of her mind had been the hope that somehow, some day, things might be different...

After all this time she could still feel the trauma of waking up in hospital with no knowledge of who she was or how she'd come to be there, of being tended by doctors and nurses who talked over her head and treated her as though she was some inanimate object rather than a human being.

Then, as her brain had slowly cleared, she had begun to remember odd things, like scattered pieces of a jigsaw... Tony coming home from the hospital in despair... A Christmas party... Getting into the car... Driving, though heavily pregnant, because Tony had been drunk... *Pregnant*...

Beneath the white sheet, her hands felt the flatness of her stomach. Panic-stricken, she cried hoarsely, 'Nurse... Nurse...'

A nurse came hurrying in and bent over her. 'So you're fully conscious at last.'

'My baby,' she choked, 'what's happened to my baby?'

'Don't worry, your daughter was born safely in the hospital. She was a fine, healthy seven and a half pounds.'

Relief brought weak tears, tears that ran silently down a face which felt peculiarly stiff and alien. Tony would be so pleased... He'd wanted a girl... 'Where is she? Can I see her?'

'You weren't in any state to take care of her, so your mother-in-law took her home.'

Lifting her hands to brush away the tears, Kate's fingers encountered unfamiliar facial contours and raised scar tissue... 'What happened?'

'You were injured in a car crash, but there's nothing a spot of plastic surgery won't put right, as soon as you're strong enough.'

'Tony...my husband...where is he? Is he all right?'

The nurse shook her head and said simply, 'I'm sorry...'

'You mean he's dead?'

'I'm sorry,' the nurse said again. 'Your car skidded and hit one of the concrete supports of the overpass. He was killed instantly...'

Then he'd never even seen the baby he'd come to think of as his... Poor Tony... And poor Grace...

Through a fresh rain of tears, Kate asked, 'His mother...how is his mother taking it?'

'At first Mrs Carran was dreadfully upset, but since she's had time to come to terms with it things seemed to have improved somewhat. And of course the baby must be a great comfort to her.'

Since she's had time to come to terms with it...

Putting a hand to her head, Kate asked, 'How long have I been unconscious?'

'You had a badly fractured skull and you've been in a coma for almost five months...'

'Five months!'

'You're lucky to be alive,' the nurse said soberly. 'After hitting the bridge, the car turned over and was crushed when it rolled down an embankment. You were trapped inside with multiple injuries.

'When you were first cut free they thought you were

dead. Fortunately the paramedics rushed you to hospital because of the baby.'

So the baby she had never even seen was five months old...

'I'll let Mrs Carran know you've regained consciousness. She'll be so relieved. Though she's been unable to get in to see you, she's phoned almost every day to ask if there was any change.'

A shade awkwardly, the nurse added, 'I gather you haven't any other family? Apart from your stepbrother-in-law, that is...'

'Has he...?'

'Well, no... I understand he's been very busy.' Then she went on more cheerfully, 'But he's paying for one of the best rooms, and all your medical expenses...'

It was bitter to think she was nothing but a financial burden on a man who still hated her so much that he had never once come to the hospital to see her.

When, some two hours later, Grace came in to see her, Kate was shocked by the change in her mother-in-law. From being slight and elegant and young-looking, she was now shrunken and old and oddly nervous.

Taking Kate's hand, she whispered unsteadily, 'My dear, what can I say? Apart from the baby, the whole thing's been like a nightmare.'

Forestalling Kate's question, she added, 'I haven't brought her... The poor little thing has a cold, so I didn't think it was wise.'

Then she went on in a rush. 'The doctor tells me that now you've regained consciousness it shouldn't be too long before you can come home.'

'Is the apartment—?'

Grace shook her head. 'We let it go.' Flushing a little, she admitted, 'You were so badly injured it seemed hopeless at the time. But now a miracle's happened, and...' The words tailed off. Taking a deep breath, she asked jerkily, 'Have you any idea yet what you intend to do when you get out of hospital?'

'I haven't had a chance to think about it.'

'Please, Kate, come and live with us.'

'I'm sorry, but there's no way I can live in Matthew's house.'

'But Sara and Matt—'

'Sara?'

'Matt's fiancée... They're getting married at the end of July. I know they'd both be only too happy for you to—'

As Kate started to shake her head Grace went on desperately, 'You'll need *somewhere* to live, and you've no means of supporting a baby... It may be months yet before you're fit to work, or even take care of her...

'Oh, please don't take her away from me. You can't know how I've longed for a grandchild...' Grace began to sob harshly. 'She's all I have left now Tony's gone...'

Swallowing hard, Kate said, 'You've got Matthew...'

'It isn't the same. He was never *mine*.'

'But when he and Sara are married you'll no doubt have more grandchildren.'

'No, I won't...' Taking a deep breath, Grace scrubbed at her face with a handkerchief. 'Sara can't have any children. When she was very young and foolish she had an abortion that went wrong... But both she and Matt want a child, and if anything had happened to you, they were hoping to adopt the baby...'

Seeing her daughter-in-law's stricken face, Grace cried, her own face blanching, 'Oh, no, my dear, don't think for a moment we ever wished... We *prayed* for your recovery...'

Less than two weeks later, after days and nights of anguished thought that had sent her temperature sky-high, Kate put on her baggy maternity dress and threadbare winter coat, which had been cleaned and stored in her bedside wardrobe, and in the quiet time between staff changes walked out of the hospital.

She walked blindly, automatically, with no idea where she was going, her only thought now to put distance between herself and the luxurious room that had become a prison.

The late May evening was cool and overcast; a fine drizzle glistened on the sidewalks and produced an ozone smell as it overlaid the dust.

As usual, traffic was fairly heavy, but at this hour, when most people were home from work and the night's socialising hadn't yet begun, there were few pedestrians.

Before long the rain began to fall in earnest, cold and unrelenting, soaking through the shoulders of her thin coat. Though she was still in a traumatised state, a thread of common sense told her she needed to find somewhere for the night.

But her purse was empty, except for her credit cards, and credit cards were useless when she had no way of paying them off.

Perhaps she could book into a cheap hotel and stay for a night or two while she tried to find some kind of job?

But even as the thought crossed her mind she knew it was hopeless. She had no luggage and her clothes were shabby. People would take one look at her and turn her away.

She had walked for perhaps three-quarters of a mile through unfamiliar streets when fatigue forced her to stop and lean against a wall.

Beyond the wall was what looked like a chapel, and outside it a black noticeboard with gold lettering read, 'St Savior Mission. Morningside Heights. If you are hungry or homeless, come inside.'

It seemed to be the answer to an unspoken prayer...

*   *   *

The sound of a door closing brought Caroline back to the present, and a moment later Matthew appeared.

'Sorry to rush off like that,' he apologised, 'but the situation sounded as if it might be serious.'

'Was it?'

'Potentially, but everything's under control. The fire's out and my most experienced engineer is checking for damage and possible causes.'

Sitting down beside her, he stretched a lazy arm along the back of the settee.

She sat quite still, her heart beating fast.

Turning his head to look at her, he queried, 'What were you thinking when I came in, that made you look so lost and desolate?'

'I—I don't really remember.'

'You mean you don't want to tell me.' Mockingly he added, 'I've always considered a wife shouldn't have any secrets from her husband.'

Her heart beating even faster, she pointed out, 'I'm not your wife yet.'

'But you soon will be, and the sooner the better.'

When she made no demur, he stroked a lean finger down her cheek, making her shiver with pleasure, and commented thoughtfully, 'You don't seem to have too many qualms about marrying a man you scarcely know.'

'Should I have?'

He smiled thinly. 'I'm not planning to turn into Bluebeard.'

'I'll take your word for it,' she told him, as lightly as possible.

As if it was a warning, he added softly, 'Though I can't promise never to mix you up with Kate...'

A cold chill ran down her spine.

'Knowing that, if you're brave enough to go ahead, I'd like us to be married at the earliest possible moment. Agreed?'

She nodded.

'Then we'll go back to New York tomorrow and I'll make all the necessary arrangements. I take it that as you've been married before you'll be happy with a small, quiet ceremony?'

'Yes.'

'What about last time?'

'Last time?' Her voice betrayed her alarm.

'Did you have a big wedding?'

'No.'

'But you wore white?'

'No.'

'Where were you married? In church?'

'It was a civil ceremony,' she answered jerkily.

He nodded, as if satisfied, and his fingers slipped beneath her hair to caress her nape.

'Tell me, Caroline, what was your husband like?'

Thrown completely by Matthew's sudden question, she simply gazed at him.

A dark brow lifted. 'Surely you can't have forgotten?'

'No, I haven't forgotten,' she replied hoarsely. 'I just try not to dwell on the past.'

When she said nothing further, Matthew pursued, 'I suppose that's natural, with him dying so tragically young... Did you say he was killed in a road crash, the same as my stepbrother?'

'No...I said he had a very rare form of cancer.'

A glance at Matthew's face showed it was curiously bleak and angry.

'But I'd rather not talk about him, if you don't mind. It still upsets me.'

'After more than two years?'

'Yes.'

'That night in the house you told me you'd been "fond" of him. I take it that you still are?'

'Yes,' she answered tightly.

'Somehow mere fondness doesn't seem to be enough to engender such strong feelings...' With a gleam of self-contempt in his tawny eyes, he added, 'Now, if it had been the kind of obsession I felt—still do feel—for Kate...'

His hand moved to lift and play with the necklet. 'Shall I tell you about Kate?'

She froze. 'You already have.'

As though he hadn't heard her, he went on, 'Not that there's much to tell. Our time together was so brief. All it amounted to really was just a day and two nights. Yet I've never been free of her since. She won't let me go...'

'Perhaps it's *you* that won't let go?' The instant the words were out, Caroline could have bitten her tongue.

His green-gold eyes pinned her. 'It isn't easy to let go of something or someone you hate. Have you ever hated anyone?'

'No, I haven't,' she said shakily.

'Hatred is a very powerful emotion. The flipside of love.'

'All I know is that it can warp and destroy the person who feels it.'

'So you think I should try to stop hating her?' he queried mockingly.

When Caroline failed to respond, he pressed, 'And how would you recommend I do that?'

'Perhaps if you didn't blame her for so much,' she suggested helplessly.

'Such as what?'

'Well...for your stepbrother's death...and for abandoning Caitlin...'

His heavy lids drooped, the long thick lashes hiding the expression in his eyes. 'Why do you imagine I blame her for those?' he asked silkily.

Startled, she answered, 'Because you said so.'

'What makes you think that Tony's wife and Kate are one and the same?'

Feeling as though she had fallen down a lift shaft, she stammered, 'Wh—what?'

His voice like polished steel, he repeated the question.

'I—I thought from different things you've said...'

'I'm quite sure that I've never, at any time, indicated that they were the same woman.'

'Somehow I got the impression...I presumed... I'm sorry, I—I must have misunderstood. It was stupid of me.'

'On the contrary, it shows an almost psychic brilliance. Kate *is*, or was, my stepsister-in-law. Maybe that's what I hold against her the most. Though she was prepared to jump into bed with me, she preferred my stepbrother.'

His handsome face was full of bitterness. 'I have no doubt moralists would say that was only fair. After all, she was his before she was mine.'

As Caroline sat mute and stricken Matthew went on in a sudden change of direction. 'However, that's all in the past—something that can't be altered. We've got the future to look forward to.'

But what kind of future would it be when he was only marrying her because she reminded him of a woman he hated? Caroline wondered bleakly.

As though reading her thoughts, he added, 'Ours may not be the ideal storybook marriage, but so long as we both get what we want out of it...'

Greatly troubled, she asked, 'What do *you* want out of it?'

The anger was still there, making his sudden smile glittering and dangerous, but he answered equably enough. 'A passionate lover, a companionable wife, a mother for Caitlin and for my own children...

'And you, Caroline, what do you want out of this marriage?'

Uncomfortable now, she said awkwardly, 'A home and a family...'

'You haven't mentioned a husband.'

'That goes without saying.'

'If you could ask for one special blessing, what would it be?'

I'd ask for you to love me. A simple thing to want, but so impossible that it would be like wishing for the moon.

Aloud, she said, 'I don't really know. Perhaps the ability to be content with what one does have.'

He studied the pure lines of her profile. 'I'm marrying a philosopher, I can see.' His voice was harsh. 'And a beautiful one at that.'

The hand that had been resting on her nape moved to take her chin and turn her face to his.

Everything about him was hard and handsome: the strong bone-structure, the straight nose, the firm jaw and chiselled lips.

His expression was that of a hunter, alert and ruthless and, though hidden now, she could sense the lingering anger.

In an unconscious admission of fright, she licked her lips, and was aware that his narrowed gaze had followed the betraying movement.

Her heart began to pound rapidly. 'Please, Matthew...' Physically and emotionally drained, all she wanted was to sleep.

Ignoring her appeal, he bent his dark head.

When his mouth closed remorselessly over hers, she made a little half-choked sound, deep in her throat, and arched her body as though she was about to be tortured.

He kissed her deeply, searchingly, exploring and exploiting the sweetness of her mouth. His lovemaking was both savage and punitive. There was no tenderness there, but a kind of controlled violence, as though he had become addicted to a sweetness he despised.

Yet she knew he'd once been a sensitive lover, capable of great tenderness. If he was hard and cruel now, it was *she* who had made him that way. That was one thing she must take the blame for.

After a while his kiss, though still passionate, gentled a little, seeking and demanding a response she was unable to withhold. Her arms went around his neck and, her heart full to overflowing, she kissed him with an answering passion while his hands moved over her slender curves.

Almost instantly she was lost to everything but the pleasure of his touch. Though the evening had been fraught, she no longer felt any fear or apprehension. Neither past nor future existed, only the here and now.

When finally he whispered, his lips brushing her ear, 'Ready for bed?' she nodded, and rose gladly.

After checking on Caitlin, Matthew disappeared into the guest bathroom while Caroline went to use their *en suite* facilities to shower and prepare for bed.

Catching sight of her reflection in the mirror, she realised with a shock that she was still wearing the gold necklet.

All the traumas of the day had taken their toll, and above the burnished collar her face looked strained and drained of colour, her eyes unusually large.

Being forced to wear the necklet set her on edge. Raising both hands, she fingered each link, pushing and pulling and twisting in an attempt to find the hidden clasp.

She was unsuccessful.

But if she went hurrying to Matthew now, it would give away how much it bothered her. Better to wait until he came, and then, before they made love, ask him casually to unfasten it.

Her undies and nightclothes had been put away neatly in the chest of drawers. She found and donned her prettiest nightdress before climbing into the big divan to wait for Matthew with a singing anticipation.

When he came in nude, and slid in beside her, she turned towards him eagerly. Reaching out a lean hand, he brushed a silky strand of hair away from her cheek and, having studied her, said, 'It's been a long day. You look too weary to do anything but go to sleep in my arms.'

Perhaps he took her faint sigh to be relief, because he drew her close and settled her head on his shoulder in the age-old position of comfort.

She stirred uneasily. 'Matthew...'

'Mmm?' He glanced down at her.

'The necklet...'

'You said it wasn't uncomfortable.'

'It isn't, but I—'

'Then relax; it looks wonderful.' He kissed her gently.

But even his show of kindness couldn't quite banish her suspicion that he knew exactly what effect it was having on her, and had planned it that way.

CHAPTER NINE

THEY were married in New York City some three weeks later, in a beautiful old church incongruously sandwiched between two glass and concrete skyscrapers. Only a handful of people were present at the short, simple ceremony.

When they left the church, walking a little apart like careful strangers, it was snowing, the white, feathery flakes drifting down, taking the place of confetti.

Matthew's big four-wheel drive, with their luggage in the trunk, was waiting to take them back to Clear Lake for a short honeymoon.

The first time a honeymoon had been mentioned had been the previous evening when, coming out of his study, Matthew had said coolly, 'I thought after the ceremony we'd go up to the spa for a few days.'

With mixed feelings, Caroline had asked, 'Would you like me to pack for you?'

'Eager to practise your wifely duties?' It had been almost a sneer.

Flushing a little, she'd said, 'Not at all. If you prefer to do your own, I'll just pack for Caitlin and myself.'

'Caitlin won't be going.'

'Oh, but—'

'It isn't *usual* to take one's children on honeymoon,' he'd pointed out. 'And I had rather hoped to have my bride to myself for a few days, before we start becoming a family.'

When Caroline had said nothing, he'd added, 'Caitlin will be fine staying with Mrs Monaghan.'

151

'But will Mrs Monaghan—?'

'She's quite trustworthy, and happy to take care of the child. Even more important, Caitlin is quite happy to stay with her.' His tone had made it clear that the matter was settled.

Now, snowflakes settling on his dark hair, Matthew opened the car door and waited with distant civility while his wife got in.

As soon as she'd fastened her seat belt he slid behind the wheel and they started their silent journey upstate.

No two people could have looked, or acted, less like newlyweds, Caroline thought unhappily. At the end of the ceremony Matthew hadn't even kissed her.

But if he was regretting his precipitate proposal, and it seemed that he was, why had he gone through with the marriage?

Presumably the reasons he'd first given still stood, though until the evening before she had begun to doubt whether he even *wanted* her any longer.

After eventually falling asleep in his arms that last night at the lodge, she had awakened alone. Going in search of him, she had found him in the kitchen getting Caitlin and Barnaby their breakfast fruit and cereal.

'Good morning.' His greeting had been terse, and it was immediately obvious that the gentle mood of the previous night had been replaced by one of curt efficiency.

Even so, when they had returned to New York City later that day, she had expected him to take both cases to his room, having forced her hand over sharing his bed. Instead, without comment, he had carried hers through to her own suite next to the nursery.

At Clear Lake, apart from making sure she was wearing his ring, the ethics of the situation hadn't seemed to trouble him overmuch, but now he was at home he was apparently intent on observing the proprieties.

The first night back at the penthouse, lying awake and restless, she consoled herself with that thought. But when, during the days that followed, he immersed himself in his work, so that she saw virtually nothing of him, and it became quite clear that he was avoiding her, she started to feel hopelessly hurt and bewildered.

With Caitlin to love and look after, the days passed quickly and happily, but the sleepless nights, with only her anxious thoughts for company, seemed endless, and soon she had mauve shadows like bruises beneath her beautiful eyes.

Though he had insisted on her wearing her ring, and had personally told Mrs Monaghan of their engagement, to all intents and purposes she was back to being a nanny again, while he, cool and aloof, built an icy wall around himself that shut her out.

If it hadn't been for the ring, and the fact that he now spoke of her as 'Mummy' when he talked to Caitlin, Caroline might have thought she'd imagined his proposal.

Then, just last night, she had glanced up and caught him watching her, seen the white-hot blaze of desire in his eyes before he'd turned abruptly away.

It had been like walking past the open door of a blast furnace.

Thinking of the lonely nights they'd spent apart, she wondered dazedly if he'd been trying to prove something? Or had he simply been intent on punishing them both? Her because she reminded him of Kate; himself because he hated the obsession he was unable to free himself from.

Recognising that it irked him as much as the gold

necklet had irked her, before he'd consented to remove it, she felt desperately sorry for him.

But when he was cured of that obsession—and no doubt the time would come—where would that leave her? What was there to take its place?

Hopefully kindness, and some degree of caring... If she was his wife, and the mother of his children, surely he'd come to feel something for her?

As they travelled through the snowy evening she tried hard to hold onto that thought, but in her heart of hearts she knew that with the past hanging over them like the sword of Damocles it was unlikely they would ever find any real happiness together.

Eventually, lulled by the swish of the wiper blades and the motion of the car, she drifted into an uneasy sleep.

She had slept heavily for some time when she awoke with a start to find they had arrived at the spa. Glancing sideways, she saw that Matthew was watching her, a strange, bleak look on his face.

Before she could gather her wits, he had jumped out and come round to open her door. As she got out, still only half awake, she staggered, and he put an arm around her waist.

Apart from slipping the heavy gold wedding ring onto her finger, it was the first time he had touched her in weeks.

As they'd travelled north the sky had cleared, and now it was a beautiful night, an almost full moon riding above the pines. The earlier fall of snow, still crisp and fresh, crunched beneath their feet as they made their way up the steps and into the foyer.

Miss Deering, who was behind the desk, looked up and said a polite, 'Good evening, Mr Carran...Mrs Carran. Many congratulations!'

So they knew about the wedding, Caroline thought dazedly as one of the staff hurried out to fetch their luggage.

'If you can spare just a moment, Mr Carran,' Miss Deering added, 'the manager would like a brief word with you. He's in his office.'

Matthew nodded.

His arm still around Caroline, who was trying not to sway on her feet, he led her across to his suite and, opening the door, steered her inside.

A moment later one of the porters carried in their luggage and hurried away again.

About to follow him out, Matthew glanced back to say, 'I suggest you get straight to bed.'

Something in his manner disturbed her and made her ask anxiously, 'You *are* coming back?'

'Of course.' His dark face sardonic, he added, 'What would the staff think if I deserted you on our wedding night?' A second later the door clicked shut behind him.

By the time Caroline had hung up the soft aubergine-coloured wool suit she'd been married in, unpacked her night things, showered and climbed into bed, almost half an hour had passed and still Matthew hadn't returned.

Intent on banishing sleep, she had deliberately kept the water overly cool, and instead of lying down she picked a book from the shelves at random and sat up with the light on.

She was so tired the print danced before her eyes. But he had said he was coming back, and when he did she wanted to be awake.

Earlier, during the journey, she had wondered fearfully what would happen when eventually his obsession died. Now she was anxious about the more immediate future.

Though she was certain he still wanted her, having

seen that look of blazing desire, his self-control was awesome, and she feared it.

He'd said he wanted a family, but suppose he'd changed his mind? Suppose, hating her and despising himself, he'd made a conscious decision to keep on denying both their needs?

Until she'd had time to try and build some kind of rapport that physical bond was the only thing they shared, and if he continued to shut her out, even though she would still have Caitlin, it would be a kind of torture.

When he'd offered her the chance to be with him it had seemed like a wish come true, but hadn't some sage said, 'Be careful what you wish for—it might come true'?

Shivering, she decided that somehow she *had* to melt those walls of ice he'd surrounded himself with. If she was unable to reach him tonight, she might never be able to.

The thought terrified her.

She stirred and awoke to semi-darkness. There wasn't a sound. At first she was dazed, disorientated, unable to remember where she was.

Then it all came rushing back. She was at Clear Lake on her honeymoon, and this was her wedding night.

But where was Matthew?

Her searching hand encountered no slumbering form, though the digital clock showed it was two-thirty in the morning.

She sat up abruptly. Moonlight filtering in confirmed that the place beside her was empty, the pillow smooth and undented. It was clear that so far she'd slept alone.

But someone had been in and put her book neatly on the bedside table before switching out the light.

Looking at her wedding ring, she felt a sense of despair. She was Matthew's wife, yet not his wife.

So what was she to do? Meekly submit to whatever *he* decided? No, she had weapons, too. It was about time she began to use them.

Getting out of bed, she padded silently to the door and along the passage. There were no lights anywhere. Pausing at the door of the second bedroom, she listened. Despite the silence, instinct told her he was in there.

Opening the door, she slipped inside. Her vision had adjusted to the gloom of the passage, and the moonlight in the room seemed even brighter.

He was lying in bed, his hands clasped beneath his dark head. As she walked towards him she saw the glitter of his eyes, and caught her breath as she realised he was wide awake.

'Well, well, well...' he murmured softly, mockingly. 'If it isn't the bride.'

She fought down a cowardly impulse to turn tail and run. 'I wanted to wait for you, but I must have fallen asleep...' Her voice as casual as she could make it, she added, 'When I woke up, I wondered where you'd got to.'

When he said nothing, she decided to take the bull by the horns and asked, 'Why did you choose to sleep in here?'

'I got to thinking about your first marriage. I've always disliked...shall we say...second-hand merchandise...'

Knowing he was trying to hurt her, she lifted her chin. 'It didn't stop you making love to me before we were married.'

From his expression, she saw he hadn't expected her to fight back.

Curtly, he said, 'I suggest you return to bed before you get cold.'

Remembering that blazing look, she clung to the coat-tails of her rapidly disappearing courage. 'I'm already cold...'

She was standing in a patch of moonlight that made the thin material of her nightdress almost transparent and proved the truth of her words.

'I was hoping you would warm me like you did in your house that night.'

His voice roughening, he advised her, 'I'm warning you, Caroline, if you don't go right now, you may get more than you bargained for.'

'I'll chance it.'

'Very well.' His teeth snapping together, he ordered, 'Take it off.'

'What?'

'The nightdress. Take it off. If you're determined to stay, you won't need it.'

She hesitated only briefly, then, slipping the thin straps from her shoulders, she allowed the garment to fall around her feet and stood slim and straight while the moonlight turned her into a silver statue.

When, his eyes fixed on her, he neither moved nor spoke, she stepped out of the puddle of material and slipped into bed beside him.

He was lying unnaturally still and rigid, and, afraid he was about to change his mind and order her back to her room, she reached out boldly to touch him, running a caressing hand over his chest and flat stomach.

Hearing the hiss of his indrawn breath, she moved so that his body was half supporting hers and began to press kisses along the smooth skin of his shoulder, before nuzzling her face against his throat and touching the warm hollow with her tongue-tip.

Still he lay quite still, and she reached to plant soft butterfly kisses along his firm jaw, feeling the faint rasp of stubble. Even when her lips touched his, and lingered enticingly, he made no move to return her kiss. In one last gamble, she took his lower lip between her teeth and bit him delicately.

When he failed to respond to the deliberate provocation, she was about to turn away realising with despair that she'd lost, when all at once, with a sound almost like a growl, he rolled, pinning her beneath him.

Giving no quarter, his hands clamped down on her upper arms and his mouth sought her breast. She gasped as it closed over a firm nipple and began to suckle, lips and teeth and tongue causing needle-sharp sensations that were so exquisite as to be almost painful.

There was a recklessness about him, a hint of savagery that should have scared her, but all she could feel was triumph as a combination of passion and anger melted that icy control.

Gone was the gentle, considerate lover—in his place a man who had been pushed to the limits of his endurance.

Without any preliminaries, his mouth still at her breast, he took her with a fiery, uncontrolled passion.

He made no concessions, and she asked for none. She met him as an equal, her passion rising to meet and match his, and, holding nothing back, gave all she had to give.

Perhaps this time he had only intended to *take*, but how can one take what is given freely, generously?

Afterwards, when his dark head lay heavy on her breast, she cradled it to her with a heartbreaking tenderness, while tears of thankfulness ran silently down her cheeks.

And when, a little while later, they both drifted into

sleep, for the first time in their relationship she was holding him.

She awoke to find bright morning sun taking the place of moonlight. Filtering through the curtains, it lay like a thin layer of gold-dust on the polished wood floor.

For a moment she lay quite still, then slowly turned her head. She was alone and, if the chill of the sheets was anything to go by, had been for some time.

She got out of bed and, gathering up the discarded nightdress, hurried into the other bedroom. Wanting to see Matthew, to gauge his mood, she showered and dressed quickly, and as soon as she had brushed her long hair, leaving it loose, she went through to the living-room, her heart beating fast.

Would he smile at her, or would he look at her coldly?

It came as a complete anticlimax when there was no sign of him. The whole place was quiet. Disappointed, she made herself a cup of instant coffee and a slice of toast.

The clock showed almost ten-thirty, so Matthew, who was an early riser, had probably been up for hours.

Perhaps he'd gone out?

No, if only for the look of the thing, he wouldn't have gone out without her. His absence was more likely to be something to do with the running of the spa.

Feeling as if she needed some exercise, Caroline thought longingly of the pool area. When Matthew got back she might suggest going for a swim. Though she would have to take care not to look too competent.

When more than an hour had passed, with no sign of him, impatient now, vexed that he was treating her like this when it was supposed to be their honeymoon, she went out to the reception desk and asked as casually as possible, 'Do you happen to know where my husband is?'

'I'm sorry, I don't, Mrs Carran,' the girl said. 'But if you like I'll ring round and try to track him down for you.'

'Oh, no, thanks,' Caroline refused hastily. 'It's not important.'

After another half an hour of fruitless waiting, she found her costume and robe and a pair of flat sandals, and, her temper rising, made her way to the pool area and changed as quickly as possible.

Trying to banish everything from her mind but the pleasure she was anticipating, Caroline headed for the Olympic-sized lagoon pool, with its deep water and waves.

She was almost there when she was overtaken by a well-built man with fair hair. He was wearing flip-flops and a short terry-towelling robe over blue swimming trunks. A pair of Perspex goggles were thrust into one pocket.

As he passed he glanced her way, and his handsome face broke into a smile. 'Well, hi there! Miss Hunter, isn't it? No, I guess it's Mrs Carran now,' he corrected himself.

It took her a second or two to recognise Brett Colyer, her swimming instructor. Returning his smile, she said, 'Hi…are you on duty?'

'It's my afternoon off.' He grinned boyishly. 'So would you believe I'm taking a busman's holiday? Are you intending to swim, or just laze by the pool?'

'I'm intending to swim.'

'Alone?'

'Yes,' she admitted. Then, seeing his look of doubt, she fibbed, 'I've had a bit of practice since you saw me last.'

'So how's it going?'

'Not bad at all,' she said lightly.

Sounding a shade concerned, he asked, 'But you weren't planning to go in the lagoon?'

'Yes, I thought I would.'

He frowned. 'It's really only for experienced swimmers, and at the moment there's no lifeguard on duty.'

Clearly he was a nice man, who took his job seriously. Wanting to tell him she *was* experienced, but knowing she couldn't, she promised, 'Well, I'll certainly be careful.'

'I don't like the idea of you going in by yourself,' Brett said awkwardly. 'It's lunchtime and there aren't many people about. I think I should come in with you.'

'There's absolutely no need for you to worry.'

Sounding even more uncomfortable, he asked, 'Can I ask you something? Does Mr Carran know that you're swimming alone?'

'Well, no, but...'

'Look, Mrs Carran, I don't want to push my company onto you, but if I let anything happen to you your husband would never forgive me.' Humorously, he added, 'And I'd rather not be out of a job.'

Annoyed that her freedom was gone, but recognising that she'd dug herself into a hole, Caroline gave in gracefully. 'It seems a shame to have to spend your free time nursemaiding the boss's wife, but if it will make you happier...'

'It sure will.' He beamed his relief.

'Then I'll be glad to have your company.'

He glanced at his watch. 'It's turned one o'clock... Were you planning to have a spot of lunch first?'

'Have you eaten yet?'

He shook his head. 'I was going to get a snack at the lagoon bar.'

'Then let's do that. Oh...'

'Something wrong?'

'I don't have any money with me.'

'No problem,' he assured her. 'I'll put it on my bill.'

Having accepted that her afternoon had been ruined, she found that lunch turned out to be a pleasant surprise. Always in Matthew's company there was a certain stress factor present, but Brett was open, uncomplicated and entertaining, and Caroline found herself enjoying his easy, undemanding companionship.

'How did you become a swimming instructor?' she asked, during a lull in the conversation.

'Quite by chance,' he admitted. 'I started to train to be a doctor, but my mother fell ill and needed my help, so after a couple of years I was forced to leave medical school.

'It was just about the time the spa opened. Swimming has always been my sport, so I jumped at the chance of coming here...'

Their light lunch over, she said, 'Perhaps I'll have that dip now. Then, once you've seen me safely out, there'll still be time for you to get a spot of serious swimming in.'

They were making their way across the end of the pool, where real rocks ran down to the water, when without warning a couple of youths, one chasing the other, came running past.

The second one bumped into Caroline and knocked her off balance. Her sandalled foot slipped on the wet rock and she took a nasty tumble. Brett shouted furiously but ineffectually after the pair.

'Blasted idiots!' he stormed. 'They should be a damn sight more careful.' Then he added with concern, 'Are you all right?'

Though badly shaken, she managed, 'Yes, I'm all right.'

But as he helped her to her feet she gave a murmur

of pain. 'What is it?' he asked urgently. 'What have you done?'

'I've hurt my shoulder,' she admitted, 'and my arm's gone dead.'

Brett muttered something under his breath. Aloud, he said, 'Look, my room's just through those glass doors marked "Staff Only" and across the passage. If you can make it there, I can check the extent of the damage and, should it prove necessary, ring for your husband.'

Though his room was quite close, by the time they'd reached it Caroline was having to bite her lip.

'Pretty painful, huh?' Brett commented sympathetically.

'My arm's starting to hurt now, but I don't think I've broken anything.'

'I certainly hope not...' Opening the door into a comfortable bedsitter, he helped her inside. 'But I'd better take a look—especially at that shoulder. It could be dislocated.'

A supportive arm still around her, he suggested, 'Let me help you off with the robe before you—'

The sentence was never finished. Just as he began to ease the robe from her shoulders the door suddenly burst open and Matthew strode into the room.

Absorbing the little scene at a glance, his face turned to a white mask of fury. 'Take your hands off my wife.' The order, though quiet, cut like a whiplash.

'Brett was only—' Caroline started to protest.

Seizing her wrist, Matthew set off for the door. When he reached it he turned to say with a kind of raging calm, 'You'd better pack and get off the complex, Colyer, before I'm tempted to break your neck.'

'But, Matthew, you don't understand—'

At the same moment Brett said, 'Mr Carran, if you'd

let me explain... We were just going for a swim when your wife was involved in an accident and I—'

'You heard what I said,' Matthew growled. 'If you haven't gone by the time I get back I won't be responsible for my actions.'

The door closed decisively behind them, and, her wrist in a vice-like grip, Caroline was hurried along the staff corridor. To her very great relief they met nobody.

By the time they reached their suite she was breathless, and her forehead was dewed with cold perspiration.

As the door banged shut behind them she pulled herself free and cried, 'How dare you manhandle me?'

A dangerous gleam in his eye, Matthew said with quiet fury, 'I've a good mind to put you over my knee.'

'But I haven't done anything, and neither has Brett.' Suddenly close to tears, she choked, 'How *could* you treat him like that? He's a kind, caring man, and—'

'Was that why you went running to him the minute I turned my back?'

'I did no such thing,' she denied. 'We met by the pool quite by accident.'

'Spare me the excuses.'

'Matthew, please listen,' she begged, sinking down on the nearest chair. 'Brett was only trying to help. He was concerned that I wasn't a good enough swimmer. All he did was offer to come in the pool with me and—'

'You had lunch together.'

'Yes, but—'

'And not long afterwards I find you in his room and him helping to undress you.'

'Oh, don't be ridiculous!' she burst out crossly.

The words ended in a little cry of pain as, striding forward, Matthew seized her upper arms and yanked her to her feet. 'You little bitch,' he snarled. 'I might have known that whether you were calling yourself Kate or Caroline you hadn't changed.'

The shock was chaotic, making her heart lurch and robbing her of breath.

Seeing her face turn chalk-white, he taunted, 'Did you think I didn't know? You may have changed your appearance, but those eyes are unmistakable. You can't alter those. Nor your character.'

He laughed harshly. 'Didn't I satisfy you last night? Couldn't you wait until tonight to see if I could do any better?'

When, her very lips bloodless, she failed to answer, he said, 'Obviously not. You had to grab the first man that came along. You were a tramp when I first met you and you're still a tramp.'

'That's not true.'

'If I'd been another minute or so I would have found—'

'You would have found Brett Colyer—who, incidentally, is a better, kinder human being than you'll ever be—checking for possible injuries. I've hurt my arm, and he thought my shoulder might be dislocated.'

'What?' Matthew demanded.

He let go of her and she sank back onto the chair.

Despite the pain that was making her feel sick, she lifted her chin and looked him in the eye. 'We both tried to tell you I'd had an accident, but you wouldn't listen. You're so full of blind prejudice you chose to believe the worst.

'I don't mind so much for myself, I've come to expect it, but Brett only acted from the very best motives. He went out of his way to look after me...'

'I'm sure he did,' Matthew agreed silkily.

Ignoring the sarcasm, she ploughed on, 'Don't forget he didn't know I was an experienced swimmer, and I could hardly tell him. He asked if you knew I was planning to swim alone, and when I admitted you didn't, he said, "Look, Mrs Carran, I don't want to push my company onto you, but if I let anything happen to you your husband would never forgive me…"

'He did his best to take care of me,' she cried passionately, 'and this is the thanks he gets.'

His face set, the skin stretched tight over the strong bone structure, Matthew said, 'You'd better tell me what happened.'

'I *tried* to tell you, but you wouldn't listen.'

'I'm listening now. And it had better be good.'

Doing her best to keep her voice steady, she told him, leaving nothing out.

Matthew heard her out in silence, his expression shuttered. Then, his voice grim, he said, 'I'd better take a look at that arm.'

She lifted a hand to push the towelling robe aside.

'Let me.' Crouching on his haunches, he carefully removed it from her shoulders.

When he saw the extent of the bruising, she heard the breath hiss through his teeth.

Then he began to curse softly, viciously. 'I'd like to get hold of the young idiots responsible for this.'

'It was an accident,' she said shakily.

'An accident that should never have happened. If they'd been obeying even the most elementary rules—'

He broke off, and she watched him visibly fight to regain his self-control. When he'd succeeded, he finished examining her arm and shoulder, his touch gentle.

'Well, your shoulder isn't dislocated, thank the Lord, but it's no doubt painful enough to stop you doing anything too active.'

He rose to his feet and went to the wall-unit, to return a moment later with a box of medical supplies. As he bathed the area with wych-hazel she asked, 'So, are you satisfied?'

'Satisfied?' He looked startled.

'That Brett and I weren't about to...shall we say...have a roll in the hay?'

His mouth a thin, hard line, Matthew said, 'It seems in this instance I was wrong. But anyone who knows what you're really like would have jumped to the same conclusion.'

'Except that you don't know what I'm really like. You never have.'

'Well, my darling wife, as I don't intend to let you out of my sight for the rest of our honeymoon, you've got plenty of time to tell me.'

Looking at his derisive face she felt a sense of despair. She could *tell* him, but could she ever make him believe her?

CHAPTER TEN

DELAYED shock had set in, and despite the background heating and the glowing log fire Caroline had started to shiver uncontrollably.

'You'd better get out of that swimsuit and put some clothes on,' Matthew instructed.

He disappeared into the bedroom, to return after a moment with some fresh undies and a soft, loose house-coat.

When he'd helped her into them, and settled her on the couch in front of the fire, he said, 'The next priority is a hot drink and a couple of painkillers.'

'I don't agree.'

A dark eyebrow raised, he glanced questioningly at her.

'I think the next priority is to contact Brett and stop him leaving.'

For a moment Matthew looked furious, then he picked up the phone. 'Colyer, this is Matthew Carran. I believe I owe you an apology... Yes, she's fine, thanks. I'll come along and talk to you later.'

He replaced the receiver and disappeared into the kitchen, to return a few minutes later with a tray of tea and a bottle of aspirin.

When, after watching her swallow a couple of the tablets, he took a seat opposite and picked up his own cup, Caroline asked curiously, 'How did you knew where to find me?'

'When I got back, the receptionist mentioned that you'd been looking for me. She added that you'd gone

towards the pool area carrying what looked like swimwear.

'I was walking around the various pools when I
bumped into one of the staff, who asked if I was looking
for you. When I said I was, he mentioned that he'd seen
you and Colyer lunching together.'

Matthew's expression hardened. 'A moment later,
quite by chance, I happened to see the pair of you disappearing through the doors to the staff quarters. I presumed you'd been feeling neglected.'

Knowing she had nothing to lose, Caroline hit back.
'If I had been, you could hardly blame me. This is supposed to be our honeymoon and you've been treating
me like...like something of no account.'

'Which is exactly what you are.'

She flinched, as though the pain was physical. 'If you
think so little of me, why did you marry me?'

'Because Caitlin needs a mother,' he answered flatly.
'The day you came for that interview I watched your
eyes fill with tears when you saw her. It was enough to
make me think you might perhaps have earned a second
chance.'

He got up to refill their cups, and when he returned
to his seat she asked, 'After avoiding me all morning,
why did you come looking for me?'

His face tightened. 'I wasn't avoiding you. There was
a problem I had to sort out.'

All at once Caroline found herself having to stifle a
yawn.

'You look shattered,' he remarked flatly. 'When those
painkillers have had time to take effect you'd better lie
down and try to sleep for a while.'

Yes, she felt shattered, but her mind was too full of
anxious thoughts to allow her to sleep. There were things
she wanted to know, things she needed to ask.

Plucking up courage, she began, 'Matthew...how long have you known I was Kate? I thought if you knew, you would...' She faltered, and passed her tongue-tip over dry lips. 'Did you recognise me from the start?'

'I didn't recognise you at all. Except for those eyes. But I knew who you were even before you came for the interview. I arranged the whole thing.'

Her heart began to thump heavily. '*How* did you know?'

'When the hospital informed me that you'd walked out, I was furious. I hired a firm of private detectives to try and trace you, but you seemed to have disappeared off the face of the earth.

'They might never have managed to track you down if you hadn't kept your credit cards. Though you didn't use them much, you did notify the companies of your change of address. By that time you were nanny to the Amesburys' children.

'I decided to bide my time, and instructed the detective agency to monitor the situation. Six months ago they came up with the news that the Amesburys were moving back to California.

'At first I didn't know whether they were intending to take you with them. That could have caused problems...'

'Problems?' Her fine brows drew together in frown.

Cold green eyes looked straight into hers. 'I had no intention of letting you go.'

A shiver ran through her as he went on evenly, 'It was a month or so after Grace died that I was given a definite date for the move and told they were leaving you behind.

'As luck would have it, by that time I needed a nanny. I arranged for a mutual acquaintance, Sally Danvers, to contact Mrs Amesbury and virtually offer you the job.

'I didn't know if you'd have the nerve to come. It

obviously depended on whether you'd had a change of heart, and how much you wanted to see your daughter.

'Although it was nearly four years since we'd seen each other, I was expecting you to have taken some steps to alter your appearance. But when you walked in I was badly shaken. I thought for an instant that the detective agency had made a mistake and you were totally the wrong woman.

'It didn't take me long to discover that, in spite of your altered looks, the chemistry between us was as strong as ever... But still, to convince myself, I needed to see your eyes...'

She drew a deep, ragged breath, remembering how he had leaned forward and lifted the heavy glasses from her nose. 'Did you—?'

But noting the slump of her shoulders, her look of white-faced exhaustion, he rose to his feet and broke in firmly, 'No more questions until you've had a rest.'

The thought of lying down was a welcome one, but she was reluctant to leave the fire.

As though reading her mind, he said, 'If you don't want to go to bed, you should be comfortable enough on the couch. Let me give you a hand.'

He helped her to lie down and, when she was settled on her good arm, brought a blanket to tuck round her.

With so much on her mind she doubted if she would sleep. Still, it was a relief to stretch out and close her eyes.

She could feel the warmth of the fire on her face and hear the rustle of the logs as they burnt and settled, and the faint ticking of the ormolu clock...

When she stirred and opened her eyes, it was to find Matthew sitting quietly watching her.

Struggling into a sitting position, she asked, 'How long have I been asleep?'

'Almost three hours. I was beginning to think you were settled for the night. How do you feel?'

'Much better.' And it was the truth. The long sleep had rested and refreshed her.

'How about the shoulder?'

'A bit sore. No more.'

'Hungry?'

'Ravenous.'

'I'll ask for a meal to be sent in.'

'I'd like to tidy myself up before we eat.'

'Do you need any help?'

'No, thanks, I'll be fine.'

She made her way to the bathroom, noting with relief that though she could still feel the bruising it was considerably less painful.

When she got back, a dinner trolley was waiting in front of the fire, and, while the greyish-white ash from the logs fell through the bars and settled with barely a whisper, they ate in a silence loud with unspoken thoughts.

As soon as they'd done justice to the excellent fare, Matthew moved the trolley and settled Caroline on the couch once more.

Sitting in an armchair, he studied her for a moment or two before asking, 'Tell me, what made you decide to have your face altered?'

When she just looked at him blankly, he went on, 'Why did you have cosmetic surgery?'

'Because the accident broke my nose and left me terribly scarred...'

Surely he must have known? So why was he staring at her as though he couldn't believe his ears?

'I would never have been able to afford plastic surgery, but while I was staying at the Mission I—'

'Mission?' he interrupted sharply. 'What Mission?'

'The St Savior Mission. Morningside Heights.'

'What in heaven's name were you doing staying at a place like that?'

Her tone flat, dispassionate, holding not the slightest trace of self-pity, she explained, 'When I left the hospital I had no money and nowhere to go. They had a board saying, "If you are hungry or homeless, come inside". It was raining, and I was desperate, so I went in.

'I was quite ill for several weeks, but they gave me a bed and took care of me. They were absolutely wonderful...' For the first time her voice was unsteady.

Swallowing hard, she went on, 'The Amesburys helped to support the Mission. That was where I first met them. Mr Amesbury, who's a brilliant plastic surgeon, as well as a very humane man, took pity on me and fixed my face for nothing.'

'So that's how you came to be working for the Amesburys...' Matthew muttered.

Then, his eyes angry, he demanded, 'If you were as desperate as you say, why didn't you come to me?'

Quietly, she said, 'I'd rather have died than go crawling to a man who hated and despised me. When I discovered that you were paying my hospital bills, it made it feel like a prison.'

His eyes flashed. 'But no doubt a luxurious one?'

'Luxurious or not, I hated it!'

Sarcastically, he said, 'Then you did pretty well to stay there for as long as you did.'

'I didn't have much option. When I woke up they told me I'd been in a coma for almost five months.'

She watched him turn to stone, before he ordered curtly, 'Say that again.'

'They told me I'd had a badly fractured skull and been in a coma for almost five months.'

'What kind of fairy story is that?'

Staggered by his fury, she stammered, 'B-but surely you knew?'

'No one knew anything about you being in a coma.'

'Grace knew.'

'Grace knew?' He sounded thunderstruck. 'Then why the hell didn't she say anything? All she told me was that you'd suffered multiple injuries.'

'I don't know why she didn't say anything,' Caroline admitted helplessly. 'The nurse said she'd phoned almost every day to see if there was any change. When I finally regained consciousness, they let her know, and she came in to see me.'

'And you say you'd been in a coma for nearly *five months*?'

'If you don't believe me you can always check with the hospital. I dare say it will be on record.'

After a moment, as though thinking aloud, he said, 'If you weren't conscious when Caitlin was born, that explains why you didn't realise it was her birthday. I thought it was because you didn't care enough.'

His jaw tight, he ordered, 'Tell me about it.'

'When I first came to I didn't know who I was or where I was. Then things began to filter back. I remembered being pregnant, and driving home that night...

'I asked about my baby. They said she'd been born in the hospital, and she was fit and healthy... I wanted to see her, but they told me that Grace had taken her home because, being in a coma, I couldn't look after the child.'

His face white and set, Matthew said hoarsely, 'And all those months Grace gave me the impression that she was taking care of the baby simply because you didn't feel up to it.'

Then he demanded sharply, 'You said she came in to see you? Did she bring the baby?'

'No. She said the poor little thing had a cold. I was bitterly disappointed.'

'So when did you first see the child?'

'That day at your penthouse.'

Matthew muttered something that sounded like, 'Dear God.' After a moment, he urged, 'Go on.'

'When they first told me it was a girl I was so pleased. Tony had wanted a girl. I asked if he was all right... That was when they broke the news that he'd died in the crash without ever knowing...'

Seeing her eyes fill with tears, Matthew asked harshly, 'Did you really care about him and the baby?'

'Yes, I cared.' Her quiet answer was more telling than any amount of protestations. 'Just for an instant I wished I'd died with him. Then I thought about the baby and was glad I hadn't...'

'How can I believe you?' Matthew sounded tortured. 'You've told so many lies. When I asked about your husband, you said he died of cancer.'

'I said he *had* cancer, and that was the truth. He'd been feeling ill and exhausted for weeks—'

'Grace thought he was suffering from anaemia.'

'That's what he told her. He didn't want her to worry about him...

'The day of the accident he'd been to the Groober Hospital to hear the results of some tests they'd done. They told him he had less than three months to live. He came home totally shattered.

'We talked for a while, then he said he was going to a Christmas party we'd been invited to. I wanted him to get a cab, but he insisted on taking the car. His breath already smelt of bourbon, so I decided to go with him.

'When the party broke up, though he'd been drinking heavily all night—and if you don't believe me you can ask the people who gave the party—he got behind the wheel and insisted on driving home. I managed to persuade him to move over so I could drive...'

Lifting a white, pinched face, she admitted, 'But I forgot to remind him to fasten his seat belt, so in a sense you were right when you said I was to blame for his death.'

Matthew shook his head. 'I should never have said that. It wasn't only cruel, it was unforgivable. But because I'd been hurt so much myself, I was looking for ways to hit back.'

There was a long silence. She watched the firelight flicker on his face, throwing the strong bone structure into relief and shadowing his eyes.

After a while, glancing at her, he said almost wearily, 'There's one thing I don't understand... If you cared about the child, why did you take off and leave her?'

'At the time I did what I thought was best for everyone.'

'For *everyone*?' His voice was brittle. 'Are you sure you don't mean for yourself?'

'I didn't want to leave her, but, as Grace pointed out, I had no means of supporting a baby, and it might have been months before I was fit to work or even take care of her...

'The worst thing was, I had no roof over my head. Grace told me she'd let the apartment go.'

Caroline clenched her hands together. 'After the doctor had spoken to her, and said I could go home before too long, she was upset because—'

His head jerked up quickly, angrily. 'Do you mean to say she didn't *want* you to come home?'

'No, I don't mean that at all. She begged me to go and live with her. She told me that you were getting married in a couple of months, and tried to convince me that both you and your fiancée would be only too happy to have me there. She was dreadfully upset when I refused.'

'If it meant a home for you and your baby, why did you refuse?' Then he went on bitterly, 'No, don't tell me. I can guess. Because it was *my* house... I didn't realise you hated me quite so much.'

She shook her head. 'It was the other way around. I couldn't bear to be beholden to a man who hated *me*.'

'So for the sake of your damned pride you abandoned your child!'

'It wasn't just that... There were other reasons...'

'Such as?'

Bleakly, she said, 'I saw only too clearly that no one had expected me to get better, and that my regaining consciousness, far from being a blessing, had upset everything...'

'I don't know what you mean,' he denied roughly.

'When Grace found I had no intention of living in your house, she burst into tears and begged me not to take the baby away from her, she said, "You can't know how I've longed for a grandchild... She's all I have left now Tony's gone..."

'I said that when you were married she'd no doubt have more grandchildren. It was then she told me about Sara...'

'What about Sara?'

'That she couldn't have children.'

Matthew sat quite still. 'What *exactly* did Grace say?'

Alarmed by the steely look on his face, Caroline hesitated.

'Don't you remember?'

'Yes, I remember.' That conversation with her mother-in-law would be engraved on her mind if she lived to be a hundred.

'Grace said, "Sara can't have any children. When she was very young and foolish she had an abortion that went wrong... But both she and Matt want a child, and if anything had happened to you, they were hoping to adopt the baby..."'

'That was when I realised it might have been better if I'd just quietly died.'

'Don't say such a thing!'

'It was how I felt at the time.'

Matthew cursed under his breath, then said sombrely, 'Grace lied to you. There was absolutely no reason why Sara and I shouldn't have had a family.'

'B-but I don't understand,' Caroline stammered. 'Why should she lie about a thing like that?'

'For the same reason she lied to me. She led me to believe that you didn't want the child...

'Sara and I had talked about adoption simply to make sure the baby had a secure home and a safe future...

'It seems obvious now that Grace lied to all of us because she couldn't bear to part with Tony's child.

'As she saw it, the only way she could make certain the baby was never taken away from her was for you to give it up and me to adopt it...

'Leaving the hospital and disappearing without trace, as you did, was playing right into her hands...'

Matthew sighed deeply. 'However, the main share of the blame must rest on my shoulders. If I'd come to see you, or made proper enquiries, I would have known the truth and none of this would have happened. But I left it to Grace, and believed what she told me...'

His eyes darkened. 'Now you know the score, I imagine you must hate her?'

Caroline looked inwards and found nothing but a deep compassion. 'I can't bring myself to hate her. She worshipped Tony, and losing him must have broken her heart.'

As it had broken hers to leave her baby.

Apparently reading that unspoken rider, Matthew said, 'Even if you swallowed her story about Sara, I still find it difficult to believe that you were willing to let me have your baby when you wouldn't even set foot in my house... Presumably you did it because she was Tony's child?'

Caroline shook her head. 'No, that wasn't the reason.'

His eyes on her face, Matthew waited.

Knowing the time had come to tell him the truth, but unsure of how he'd take it, she began obliquely, 'When I said I wasn't going to marry Tony, I meant it—'

'I know that,' Matthew broke in. 'I went to your room early the next morning and read the note you'd left for him, where you said, "You have to believe that I can't marry you, and remember that I never said I would..."'

'I realised you'd been telling the truth, that there had been no engagement.'

She sighed. 'But by that time you didn't care?'

'Oh, yes, I cared. I decided that when I'd given Tony time to get over things, I'd come looking for you...'

Feeling as though she'd been stabbed through the heart, Caroline gazed at him.

'Fool that I was, I thought we had something rare and special. Imagine how I felt when, a few weeks later, he announced that you were getting married after all... Why did you change your mind?'

She took a deep, uneven breath. 'For two reasons...'

'I think I can guess one of them. You agreed to the marriage because you were already pregnant.'

'Yes,' she admitted. 'How did you know?'

'You'd only been married seven months when the accident happened, but you gave birth to a full-term baby...

'If you hadn't intended to marry Tony,' he added with a sudden black bitterness, 'you should have been a great deal more careful.'

Her voice just above a whisper, she admitted, 'Caitlin isn't Tony's child.'

Matthew's head came up, and, his eyes glacial, he asked, 'Then whose child is she? Or don't you know?'

Caroline clenched her hands until the knuckles gleamed white. 'Yes, I know. She's yours. That was the reason I was prepared to let you have her.'

She watched him absorb the shock, and then that rapier-sharp brain begin to check the credibility of her statement. 'The time's about right, but how can you be sure she's mine if you were jumping into bed with both of us?'

'You were the only man I'd been to bed with.'

He looked shaken. 'If that's the truth, Tony would have known the baby wasn't his. Or did you hide the fact that you were pregnant?'

'No, he knew I was pregnant. He also knew the baby wasn't his. Though he didn't know *whose* it was.'

'And he was still willing to marry you? God he must have been besotted!'

Then with rising fury he went on, 'If you knew it was my baby, how *could* you go ahead and marry someone else? Especially my own stepbrother? That's the thing I can't forgive.'

'At first I refused to consider it. He kept pressing me, and that was when I told him about the baby.

'But instead of being shocked, he seemed delighted. He said, "It seems like a miracle. The answer to my prayers... We'll tell everyone the baby's mine. I'll take care of both of you. We'll be a family..."

'Still I refused, and then he told me something he'd never told anyone else. He wanted to live what he called a "normal" life, to have a home and a family...'

She was aware that Matthew was staring at her as if he'd never seen her before.

'He couldn't come to terms with his own sexuality and he was desperate to hide it, especially from his mother, who kept asking why he didn't have a girlfriend and trying to push him into marriage.

'He felt hounded, that was why he'd been so eager that I should meet her, and when I pressed him he admitted that the main reason he'd wanted to marry me was to get his mother off his back.'

'Poor devil,' Matthew muttered.

'I think the fact that his mother half suspected made her act as she did, because when we finally got married she wasn't only happy but *relieved*.'

'Yes,' Matthew said slowly, 'it fits.' Rubbing a hand across his eyes, he added heavily, 'Strange how one can miss something so obvious until it's pointed out... But what I can't understand is how Tony could have thought for one moment that such a marriage would work.'

'I asked him that question...' Caroline smiled mirthlessly. 'It seems I'd given him the impression that I was sexually cold, next door to frigid. He thought I'd be happy to settle for a home and companionship.

'When I went on refusing to marry him, on the grounds that I was only fond of him and fondness wasn't enough, he said, "It is for me, I don't want a grand passion."

'I told him I did, and he said, "Don't be silly, darling. You're far too sensible and level-headed. If anyone looked like offering you passion on a grand scale, you'd run a mile."'

Matthew smiled wryly. 'It's obvious he didn't know you at all.'

Thinking of the previous night, she flushed.

'So your marriage was a marriage in name only?'

'Yes.'

Just for an instant she saw a look of almost savage satisfaction cross his face, then, his voice controlled but curious, he asked, 'What made a woman like you settle for such an empty existence?'

'I felt desperately sorry for him, and it seemed to be a way out for both of us.'

'What if you'd met someone else and fallen in love?'

She half shook her head.

'It's not impossible.'

'I knew I'd never fall in love.'

'Why not?'

Instead of answering, she asked, 'When I was in hospital, why did you never come and see me? Was it because you still hated me?'

'I tried to tell myself that was the reason, but the truth was I couldn't bear to. I was too hurt and angry and jealous. I couldn't forgive you for preferring Tony to me, for having his baby...'

Caroline drew an uneven breath. If he was still jealous of the past, surely he must feel something for her?

'To try to get you out of my mind I worked all the hours God sent, and spent as much time as possible away on business. If I'd known you were lying there in a coma...' His dark head dropped into his hands.

She got up a little stiffly and went to him. 'Don't blame yourself. It was my fault in the first place. If I'd told you about Tony when you first asked if there was anyone special in my life…

'But I was afraid of, well…upsetting things. I knew then that no matter what happened between us I couldn't get engaged to Tony. That's why I carried on to New York, to break it off once and for all…'

'If only I'd believed you.' He sounded like a man in torment.

She tried to push the darkness away. 'It's all in the past, over and done with. There's the future to look forward to.'

His hands dropped to his sides and he lifted his head. 'Oh, yes, the future,' he said sombrely. 'Blackmailed into marriage with a man you didn't want to marry just so you could be with your daughter…

'I'm forced to admit that, between us, Grace and I have done a pretty good job of wrecking your life.'

As though too restless to remain seated, he got to his feet and stood leaning against the mantelpiece. 'It's a bit late to start making amends, but you know the old adage—better late than never… If you'd prefer to leave me and take Caitlin, I'll buy you a house of your own and support you both.'

'Is that what you want?' She prayed it wasn't.

He turned his head to look at her, and just for a second his anguish showed. 'No, it's not… But now it has to be what *you* want.'

'Well, unless there isn't any option, I don't particularly care for the idea of being a one-parent family. I think Caitlin should have a father, and I'd certainly like a husband.'

His jaw tight, he said, 'Well, if, in the future, you fall

in love with someone you want to marry, I'll give you a divorce.'

She shook her head. 'A minute or so ago when I said I knew I'd never fall in love, you asked why not. Well, now I'll tell you...'

Every muscle in his body tense, he waited.

'You were the first man I'd ever gone to bed with, and it wasn't just sex. I fell in love with you then and I've never stopped loving you.'

He gave a kind of groan and his arms went around her. 'Are you *sure*?'

'Quite sure,' she said serenely.

His arms tightened and she gasped.

Immediately his grip loosened. 'I must be more careful,' he muttered. 'I've already hurt you enough. But after the way I've treated you, it's hard to believe...'

Seeing this usually strong, confident man needed reassurance, she told him softly, 'I knew what a chance I was taking when I came for that interview, but I couldn't stay away. And it wasn't only Caitlin I was desperate to see... You yourself recognised that the feeling between us was still there...'

'But I thought, on your side at least, it was just a strong sexual attraction.'

Suddenly breathless, she asked, 'What do you mean, "on your side at least"?'

'I mean, I took one look at you and fell hopelessly in love... I wanted to ask you to marry me the night we met, but caution suggested that I give us both some time to get to know each other first.

'However, within twenty-four hours I knew you were the wife I'd been waiting for... You had everything I'd ever hoped to find in a woman: warmth and spirit, sweetness and passion, humour and courage, and, like an unexpected gift, a bright, shining innocence.

'Then in New York the sky fell in on me. Afterwards I made myself believe that what I'd felt, was still feeling, was a kind of obsession...'

'And is that what you still believe?'

'Would you mind if it was?'

'Not so long as you spell it l-o-v-e.'

When he'd finished kissing her, he asked urgently, 'Caroline, you will stay with me?'

'How could I leave you when we're still on our honeymoon?' she teased. 'And, speaking of being on honeymoon...' Deliberately she pressed her slender body against his.

'What about your arm and shoulder?' He sounded unsure.

'Both good as new,' she assured him airily. When still he hesitated, she asked, 'Would you mind bending your head a little so I can kiss you?'

He obliged.

Against his lips, she murmured, 'If you'll help me back to the couch...? I'm feeling the need to lie down again. And it might be easier to keep warm if you were sharing it with me.'

'Are you trying to tempt me?'

'Am I succeeding?'

His voice held both joy and laughter. 'Give me a moment or two and I'll show you.'

Where were you when the storm blew in?

Snowbound

Three stormy stories about what happens to three snowbound couples, from three of your favorite authors:

SHOTGUN WEDDING by Charlotte Lamb
MURDER BY THE BOOK by Margaret St. George
ON A WING AND A PRAYER by Jackie Weger

Find out if cabin fever can melt the snow this December!

Available wherever Harlequin and Silhouette books are sold.

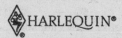 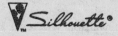

Harlequin Romance®
and Harlequin Presents®

bring you two great new miniseries
with one thing in common—MEN!
They're sexy, successful and available!

You won't want to miss these exciting romances
by some of your favorite authors,
written from the male point of view.

Harlequin Romance® brings you

Starting in January 1998 with Rebecca Winters,
we'll be bringing you one **Bachelor Territory** book
every other month. Look for books by Val Daniels,
Emma Richmond, Lucy Gordon, Heather Allison
and Barbara McMahon.

Harlequin Presents® launches **MAN TALK**
in April 1998 with bestselling author Charlotte Lamb.
Watch for books by Alison Kelly, Sandra Field and
Emma Darcy in June, August and October 1998.

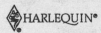 HARLEQUIN®   *There are two sides to every story...*
and now it's his turn!

HARLEQUIN WOMEN KNOW ROMANCE WHEN THEY SEE IT.

And they'll see it on **ROMANCE CLASSICS**, the new 24-hour TV channel devoted to romantic movies and original programs like the special **Romantically Speaking—Harlequin™ Goes Prime Time.**

Romantically Speaking—Harlequin™ Goes Prime Time introduces you to many of your favorite romance authors in a program developed exclusively for Harlequin® readers.

Watch for **Romantically Speaking—Harlequin™ Goes Prime Time** beginning in the summer of 1997.

If you're not receiving ROMANCE CLASSICS, call your local cable operator or satellite provider and ask for it today!

ROMANCE CLASSICS

Escape to the network of your dreams.

See Ingrid Bergman and Gregory Peck in *Spellbound* on Romance Classics.

Coming Next Month

HARLEQUIN PRESENTS®

THE BEST HAS JUST GOTTEN BETTER!

#1935 LOVESTRUCK Charlotte Lamb
Nathalie's boss, Sam, was a little the worse for wear when
he proposed to her at a party, so she decided to play along
and pretend she believed he meant it. And soon she was
really beginning to wish he *had*....

#1936 SCANDALOUS BRIDE Diana Hamilton
(Scandals!)
Nathan's whirlwind marriage was already heading for the
rocks—he was sure his wife was having an affair with her
boss! It seemed the only way to save the marriage was to
learn the truth about his scandalous bride once and for
all....

#1937 MISTRESS AND MOTHER Lynne Graham
Since separating on their wedding day, Molly maintained
that nothing could persuade her to share her husband's
bed.... Until Sholto agreed to settle her brother's debt—in
return for the wedding night he never had!

#1938 THE LOVE-CHILD Kathryn Ross
(Nanny Wanted!)
When Cathy turned up at Pearce Tyrone's villa in the south of
France, he assumed she was the nanny he'd been waiting for.
But she knew it was only a matter of time before he found
out that she wasn't all she seemed....

#1939 SECOND MARRIAGE Helen Brooks
(Husbands and Wives 2)
Claire would make the perfect bride—everyone said so. But
Romano Bellini didn't want his life complicated by a second
wife. Curious, then, that the subject of marriage just kept
coming up!

#1940 THE VALENTINE AFFAIR! Mary Lyons
Alex had promised her newspaper a Valentine exclusive on
Leo Hamilton. And after dogging Leo's all-too-attractive
heels, she realized she wanted him as an exclusive, all
right—exclusively hers!